Enid Blyton

STORIES OF
MISCHIEF
MAKERS

Look out for all of these enchanting story collections
by *Enid Blyton*

Enid Blyton

STORIES OF MISCHIEF MAKERS

Illustrations by Mark Beech

HODDER

HODDER CHILDREN'S BOOKS

This collection first published in Great Britain in 2022
by Hodder & Stoughton

1 3 5 7 9 10 8 6 4 2

Enid Blyton® and Enid Blyton's signature are registered trade marks
of Hodder & Stoughton Limited
Text © 2022 Hodder & Stoughton Limited
Cover and interior illustrations by Mark Beech. Illustrations © 2022
Hodder & Stoughton Limited

A CIP catalogue record for this book is available from the British Library.

ISBN 978 1 444 96539 1

Typeset by Avon DataSet Ltd, Alcester, Warwickshire

Printed and bound in Great Britain by Clays Ltd, Elcograf S.p.A.

The paper and board used in this book are made from
wood from responsible sources.

Hodder Children's Books
An imprint of Hachette Children's Group
Part of Hodder & Stoughton
Carmelite House
50 Victoria Embankment
London EC4Y 0DZ

An Hachette UK Company
www.hachette.co.uk
www.hachettechildrens.co.uk

Contents

Binkle Has
the Doctor

Binkle Has the Doctor

'I'M GOING down to Oak Tree Town to buy a penny stamp, Flip,' said Binkle. 'Are you coming?'

'Yes,' said Flip, reaching for his cap. 'I'm ready.'

Off the two trotted over Bumble Bee Common, down Hazel Road into Oak Tree Town.

But when they got to the Post Office, it was shut!

'Shut!' said Binkle in amazement. 'Shut! At eleven o'clock in the morning too! Fine sort of postmistress Dilly Duck is!'

Just at that moment someone walked up to the Post Office door.

'Mind, please!' said a little voice. 'I want to go in.'

'But it's shut,' said Binkle, turning round and seeing Timothy Mouse. He was carrying a steaming basin covered with a cloth.

'Of *course* it's shut!' said Timothy. 'Dilly's very ill. I'm taking her some soup my mother's made. Doesn't it smell good!'

And he went inside the Post Office and shut the door.

No sooner had he gone than someone else came up, carrying a big pink jelly on a dish.

'Good morning, Mowdie Mole,' said Binkle politely. 'Are you taking that to Dilly Duck?'

'Yes, I am. She's ill,' answered Mowdie, going into the shop.

Binkle and Flip stared at each other and sighed.

'Jelly and soup!' said Flip sadly. 'We *never* have those, Binkle.'

'And here's some flowers and grapes!' sighed Binkle, seeing Herbert Hedgehog coming up the street with his arms full.

The two rabbits went slowly home.

'Isn't it a pity one of us can't be a *little* bit ill!' said Flip.

Binkle stopped suddenly.

'That's a great idea of yours,' he said. 'One of us *will* be ill.'

'We can't be,' said Flip. 'We're both as well as can be, Binkle. Don't be silly!'

'I'm *not* silly,' said Binkle. 'I'm thinking about your idea.'

'It isn't an idea, Binkle,' groaned Flip. 'I don't have ideas. They're dangerous!'

But it was no use. Binkle was already making plans.

'Now shall you be ill, or shall I?' he wondered.

'*I'm* not going to be,' said Flip firmly, 'and I won't help *you* to be either, Binkle, and I mean that!'

'Fiddlesticks!' said Binkle rudely. 'You'll do just as I tell you, Flip. But you needn't be the ill one. I will; I should love that.'

'Oh, dear! Very well, *be* ill!' said Flip desperately,

ey went into Heather Cottage.

'I won't be ill *just* yet,' Binkle said. 'Not till Dilly's better, anyway. People can't take broth and jelly to two people at once. I'll wait for a bit and think about it.'

He waited for a week and then heard that Dilly was up and about again.

'Now's the time!' he said.

He undressed and got into bed. Flip put a clean counterpane on, and made the room look as tidy as possible.

'Oh! Oh! Oh!' groaned Binkle in bed, rolling his eyes and opening and shutting his mouth.

'What's the matter?' asked Flip in alarm.

'Nothing! I'm only just seeing if I can be ill properly,' grinned Binkle, tying a piece of red flannel round his neck. 'Now, Flip, you must do your part.'

'Part? What part?' asked Flip, his nose going up and down nervously. 'I'm not doing anything this time, Binkle.'

'Oh yes, you are,' said Binkle firmly. 'You're going to go to Sammy Squirrel the chemist, and ask him what's the best thing for a shivering fever.'

'Shivering fever! I never heard of *that*!' said Flip.

'Nor have I,' chuckled Binkle. 'He'll ask you all about it, and you can say what you like. Say I've got headaches and a cold, and I'm hot and I'm shivering and I can't sleep!'

'Oh, Binkle, you're perfectly awful!' sighed poor Flip, putting on his coat. He went off, shaking his head and wishing that Binkle wouldn't always be wanting to behave so badly.

He went to Sammy Squirrel's. There were a lot of people in the shop, but at last he got his turn.

'What's the best thing for a shivering fever?' he asked Sammy.

'Shivering fever!' exclaimed Sammy. 'What's that? Who's got it?'

'Binkle has!' explained Flip. 'He's cold and he's hot and he's got headaches.'

7

'Headaches! How many headaches has he got?' enquired Sammy with a grin.

'He's got two,' answered Flip sharply. 'One at the front and one at the back.'

'I'm sorry to hear that,' said kind Dilly Duck. 'I've just been ill myself, so I know how horrid it is. After you've got the medicine you want from Sammy, come in to me next door, Flip, and I'll give you a jelly to take to Binkle.'

Sammy gave Flip a bottle of medicine to be taken three times a day. Then Flip ran into the Post Office and Dilly gave him a yellow jelly in a big mould.

'Come and tell me how he is tomorrow,' she said. 'Has he had the doctor?'

'Er – no,' answered Flip. 'He says he won't see the doctor.'

'Dear, dear, dear, what a pity!' said Dilly, and when Flip had gone she went into Sammy's shop again and told him that Binkle wouldn't see a doctor.

'He may get terribly ill,' she said.

'Don't you worry, Dilly,' grinned Sammy. 'Binkle isn't ill; he's only pretending. Why, I saw him yesterday looking as well as ever I've seen him!'

'But, Sammy, supposing he *is* ill,' said Gillie Guinea Pig. 'It would be horrid not to be nice to him, even if he *is* always up to tricks, and behaves so badly.'

'Yes, he's a bad bunny, but if he's ill we *ought* to be nice to him – I quite agree with Gillie,' said Mowdie Mole.

Sammy thought for a minute, then his eyes twinkled.

'I'll find out for you!' he promised. 'I'll pretend I'm a doctor, and I'll go and find out. If he is really ill, we'll do our best to be kind. If he isn't – well, we'll see!'

Flip would have felt rather uncomfortable if he had known what Sammy was planning. But he didn't know – so he went on towards Heather Cottage, carrying the jelly carefully, and occasionally giving it a lick, just to see if it tasted good.

'Well?' said Binkle, when Flip came into the bedroom. 'What has happened?'

'*This* happened!' said Flip proudly, holding up the jelly. 'It's lovely! I've licked it, to see!'

The two rabbits soon finished up the jelly between them, and Flip told Binkle all that had happened. Binkle was very pleased.

'I expect lots of people will come and bring nice things,' he said hopefully. 'Do I look nice, Flip?'

'You look all right,' said Flip. 'What you've got to do isn't to look *nice* though – you've got to look *ill*!'

Nobody else called that day, and Binkle was rather disappointed.

But the next day there came a terrific rat-tat-tat on the door.

'There's somebody,' chuckled Binkle. 'Go and see who it is, Flip.'

Flip opened the door. It was someone dressed in a smart black suit, with a shiny top hat. In his paw he carried a bag.

Flip stared at him in surprise.

'I'm Doctor Curemquick,' smiled the visitor.

'Sammy Squirrel told me to come and look you up. Someone's very ill here, isn't he?'

Poor Flip didn't know what in the world to say!

'Well, Binkle isn't very well,' he stammered at last. 'He's upstairs in bed.'

'I'll go up and see him,' said the doctor, and pushing past Flip, he ran upstairs.

He walked into the bedroom and went across to the bed. Binkle stared at him in astonishment.

'It's the doctor, Binkle,' said Flip, who had followed close behind the visitor.

'*I* didn't ask any doctor to come and see me,' growled Binkle, twitching his ears nervously.

'No, Sammy Squirrel asked me to come,' said the doctor cheerfully. 'Now then, let's have a look at you! Put out your tongue!'

Binkle put out a very pink little tongue. The doctor looked at it and shook his head.

'Dear me!' he said, taking out a little notebook and writing something. 'Dear me!'

'What's the matter?' asked Binkle in alarm.

'Now take a deep breath,' said the doctor, without answering Binkle's question.

Binkle took a deep breath and the doctor tapped him hard on the chest.

'Don't do that!' said Binkle. 'You hurt me.'

'Now flap your ears up and down,' ordered the doctor, writing busily again.

Binkle did so, feeling very nervous indeed at the sight of the doctor's grave face. He began to be afraid there really must be something terribly wrong with him.

'Dear me! Dear me!' said the doctor. 'A very sad case! A – very – sad – case!'

'What's the matter with him?' asked Flip miserably, terribly upset to hear Binkle was really ill.

'Fiddle-faddlitis!' answered the doctor. 'I'll send him some medicine and some pills, and something to rub his chest with. He mustn't get up and he mustn't read. He must just lie quietly in bed and do nothing.'

'What shall I give him to eat?' asked Flip. 'Jellies and things?'

'Good gracious me, no!' said the doctor. 'Jellies and soups and things like that would kill him, in his state of health. Feed him on carrot tops mashed fine, and nothing else. I'll call again in a few days.'

He ran downstairs and out of the house. All the way over Bumble Bee Common he chuckled and chortled to himself.

'I knew he was shamming,' he said. 'This will teach him to pretend to be ill. My, what a tale to tell the others!'

And when Oak Tree Town heard how Sammy Squirrel had dressed up as a doctor and gone to see Binkle, you should have seen them smile!

But Binkle and Flip weren't smiling.

'No jellies! No soups! No broths! What's the *good* of being ill?' groaned Binkle. 'Carrot tops minced fine! Ugh!'

'Yes, this is what comes of pretending to be ill!'

scolded Flip. 'If you hadn't pretended, you wouldn't really be!'

'Don't be silly!' said Binkle, feeling that he was showing very little sympathy. 'I feel very bad, so there! Oh! Oh! Oh!'

'Don't, Binkle!' begged Flip, who was really very upset to hear Binkle was ill. 'I can't bear it. I'll do all I can for you, you know that. I'll go and get some carrot tops this very minute.'

But before he could do that, all the medicine came. Such an array there was! Boxes and bottles and jars!

Binkle tried them all. He was really afraid something was the matter with him, and he felt he ought to do all that the doctor had said.

But ugh! The medicine tasted dreadful! The pills tasted worse! And as for the stuff to rub on his chest – well, it smelt terrible!

Poor Binkle groaned and sighed at his carrot tops, and took his medicines. He didn't dare to get up, but just lay still in his bed as the doctor had ordered, feeling duller and duller each day.

Days passed, and no doctor came. Binkle had finished all the medicine and pills, and felt as if he never wanted to see a bottle again in his life.

'What's that doctor doing?' he groaned. 'Flip, go down to Sammy Squirrel's and ask him when Doctor Curemquick's coming again.'

Flip went – but, to his great astonishment, Sammy didn't seem to know anything about the doctor.

'Doctor Curemquick? Who *is* he?' he asked. 'He's never been heard of in Oak Tree Town before!'

'Well, you didn't send him then?' gasped Flip. 'What an extraordinary thing! And poor old Binkle's been taking his medicine and pills every day, and they were as nasty as could be!'

'Has he finished them?' asked Sammy Squirrel, chuckling loudly.

'Yes, every one,' said Flip. 'What are you laughing at, Sammy?'

'Oh, just thoughts,' answered Sammy, chuckling

still more loudly. 'Just my thoughts, Flip. They're rather funny!'

Flip's nose went up and down angrily.

'I believe you know more about Doctor Curemquick than you want to tell me!' he said, and stalked out of the shop and back to Bumble Bee Common.

He told Binkle that Sammy seemed to know nothing about the doctor.

'And Sammy seemed to think you being ill and having to drink medicine was a tremendous joke,' he said.

'Oh! *Oh!* OH!' yelled Binkle, suddenly jumping out of bed with a tremendous leap. 'Well, of *course* it was a joke! A joke! Oh, my stars! It must have been Sammy who dressed up as the doctor. I *thought* his face seemed a bit familiar!'

Flip's eyes opened wide.

'And he sent you all that nasty medicine – and made you stay in bed – and said you weren't to have jellies and soups!' he said. Then he suddenly began to laugh.

'It's – it's – it's very f-f-funny, Binkle,' he said, between his gurgles of laughter. 'You pretended to be ill – and *Sammy* pretended you were ill – and you thought you were and you weren't! Oh my!'

And he went off into peals of laughter again.

'Be quiet, Flip,' growled Binkle, beginning to dress himself. 'It isn't at all funny. It's a very horrid trick. It's very wrong of Sammy to pretend like that.'

'But *you* began it first,' went on Flip, chuckling loudly.

'Well, I shan't pretend any more,' roared Binkle. 'And if you don't stop laughing, I'll shove you, so there!'

But though Flip stopped laughing, Oak Tree Town didn't.

And you can't *think* how red Binkle got when anyone he met asked him if he was *really* better!

The Three Naughty Children

The Three Naughty Children

ONE DAY Queen Peronel's cook heard a knocking at her kitchen door. She opened it and saw a ragged pedlar there, his tray of goods in front of him.

'Can I sell you something?' said the pedlar. 'Red ribbons, silver thimbles, honey-chocolate, high-heeled shoes – I have them all here.'

'Nothing today, thank you,' said the cook. But the pedlar would not go.

'I am tired with walking many miles,' he said. 'Let me come in and rest a little. See, I will wipe my feet well on the mat so that I shall not dirty your clean kitchen floor.'

So the cook let him come in and sit down on her oldest chair for a little while. But when he had gone she was missing three things, and flew to tell Queen Peronel.

'Oh, Your Highness!' she cried, bursting into the drawing room where the queen sat knitting a jersey. 'Oh, Your Highness, a pedlar has stolen your blue milk jug, your little silver spoon and your wooden porridge plate! Oh, whatever shall I do!'

Now these three things were all full of magic and the queen treasured them very much. The blue milk jug had the power of pouring out perfectly fresh milk twice a day, which was very useful for the queen's nurse, for she had two little princesses and a prince to look after in the royal nursery. The silver spoon would make anyone hungry if they put it into their mouth, and this, too, was *very* useful if any of the royal children wouldn't eat a meal.

The wooden porridge plate could play a tune all the time that porridge was eaten from it, so the children loved it very much. Queen Peronel was dreadfully upset when she heard that all these things had been stolen.

'What was the pedlar like?' she asked. 'I will have him captured and put into prison.'

But alas, when the cook told her about the pedlar's looks, the queen knew that he was no pedlar but a wizard who had dressed himself up to steal her treasures. She called the king and he really didn't know what to do.

'That wizard is too powerful for us to send to prison,' he said, shaking his head. 'He won't give us back those three things if we ask him nicely, for he will say he didn't steal them. I really do *not* know what to do.'

Now when the two little princesses and the prince heard how the wizard had stolen their milk jug, porridge plate and spoon, they were very angry.

'Send a hundred soldiers to him, Father, and capture him!' cried Roland, the little prince, standing straight and tall in front of the king.

'Don't be silly, my dear child,' said the king. 'He would turn them all into wolves and send them howling back here. You wouldn't like that, would you?'

'Well, Father, send someone to steal all the things from *him*,' said Rosalind, the eldest child, throwing back her golden curls.

'You don't know what you are talking about,' said the king crossly. 'Go back to the nursery, all of you, and play at trains.'

They went back to the nursery, but they didn't play at trains. They sat in a corner and talked. Rosalind and Roland were very fierce about the stealing of their magic things. Then Roland suddenly thought of an idea.

'I say, Rosalind, what about dressing up as a wizard myself and going to call on the wizard who took away our things? Perhaps I could make him give them back. *I'm* not afraid of any old wizard!'

'I shall come too,' said Rosalind, who liked to

be in everything.

'And so shall I,' said Goldilocks, the youngest of them all.

'You're too little,' said Roland.

'I'm *not*!' said Goldilocks. 'I shall cry if you don't let me come.'

'All right, all right, you can come,' said Roland. 'But if you get turned into a worm or something, don't blame *me*!'

Then they made their plans, and very odd plans they were too. They were all to slip out of bed that night and go downstairs, dressed, when nobody was about. Roland was to get his father's grandest cloak and feathered hat, and the two girls were to take with them a pair of bellows each, a box of fireworks from the firework cupboard and two watering cans full of water. How strange!

They were most excited. They could hardly wait until the clock struck eleven and everyone else was in bed. Then they dressed and went downstairs. Soon

25

Roland was wrapped in his father's wonderful gold and silver cloak, with big diamonds at the neck and round the hem. On his curly head he put his father's magnificent feathered hat, stuffed with a piece of paper inside to make it fit. Then, with their burden of bellows, fireworks and watering cans, they set off to the wizard's little house on the hillside not far off.

It was all in darkness save for one light in the nearest window.

'He's still up,' said Roland. 'Good! Now, you two girls, you know what to do, don't you? As soon as you hear me shouting up the chimney, do your part. And if you make a mistake, Goldilocks, I'll pull your hair tomorrow, so there!'

'Help me to get the ladder out of the garden shed,' said Rosalind as they came near to the cottage. Roland and the two girls silently carried the ladder to the cottage and placed it softly against the roof. Then up went the two princesses, as quietly as cats. In half a minute they were sitting beside the chimney, their bellows, fireworks and watering cans beside them.

It was time for Roland to do his part. He wrapped the big cloak around his shoulder and strode up to the door. He hammered on it with a stone he had picked up and made a tremendous noise. The wizard inside nearly jumped out of his skin.

'Now who can this be?' he wondered, getting up. 'Some great witch or enchanter, hammering like that on my door!'

He opened the door and Roland strode in, not a bit nervous.

'Good evening, wizard,' he said. 'I am Rilloby-Rimmony-Ru, the Enchanter from the moon. I have heard that you can do wondrous things. Show me some.'

The wizard looked at Roland's grand cloak and hat and thought he must indeed be a rich and great enchanter. He bowed low.

'I can command gold to come from the air, silver to come from the streams, and music from the stars,' he said.

'Pooh!' said Roland rudely. 'Anyone can do that! Can you call the wind and make it do your bidding?'

'Great sir, no one can do that,' answered the wizard mockingly.

'Ho, you mock at me, do you?' said Roland. He went to the chimney and shouted up it. 'Wind, come down to me and show this poor wizard how you obey my commands!'

At once Rosalind and Goldilocks began to work the bellows down the chimney, blowing great puffs of air down as they opened and shut the bellows. The smoke from the fire was blown all over the room and the wizard began to cough. He looked frightened.

'Enough, enough!' he cried. 'You will smoke me out. Command the wind to stop blowing down my chimney.'

'Stop blowing, wind!' commanded Roland, shouting up the chimney. At once the two girls on the roof stopped working the bellows, and the smoke went up the chimney in the ordinary way.

'Wonderful, wonderful!' said the wizard, staring at Roland in amazement. 'I have never seen anyone make the wind his servant before.'

'That's nothing,' said Roland grandly. 'I can command the rain too.'

'Bid it come then,' said the wizard, trembling.

Roland shouted up the chimney. 'Rain, come at my bidding!' At once Rosalind and Goldilocks poured water down the chimney from their watering cans and it hissed on the fire and spat out on the hearth. The wizard leapt back in alarm.

'Stop the rain!' he cried. 'It will put out my fire if it rushes down my chimney like that.'

Roland, who didn't at all want the fire to be put out, hastily shouted to the rain to stop, and the two little girls put their watering cans down, giggling to hear the astonished cries of the wizard.

'Sure you can do no greater thing than these!' said the wizard to Roland.

'Well, I can command the thunder and lightning too,' said Roland. 'Wait. I will call down some for you to see.'

Before the frightened wizard could stop him, Roland shouted up the chimney again. 'Thunder and lightning, come down here!'

Rosalind dropped a handful of fireworks down at once. They fell into the flames and exploded with an enormous bang, flashing brightly. The wizard yelled in alarm and ran into a corner. Rosalind dropped down some more fireworks, and two squibs hopped right out of the fire to the corner where the wizard was hiding.

'Oh, oh, the thunderstorm is coming after me!' he shouted. 'Take it away, great Enchanter, take it away!'

Roland badly wanted to laugh, but he dared not even smile. Another batch of fireworks fell down the chimney and the wizard rushed away again and fell over a stool.

'Stop, thunder and lightning!' called Roland up the chimney. At once the girls stopped throwing down fireworks and there was peace and quiet in the room, save for the wizard's moans of fright.

'Am I not a powerful enchanter?' asked Roland grandly. 'Would you not like to know my secrets?'

'Oh, Master, would you tell me them?' cried the wizard, delighted.

'I will write them down on a piece of paper for you,' said Roland, 'but you must not look at it until tomorrow morning. And now, what will you give me in return?'

'Sacks of gold, cart loads of silver,' cried the grateful wizard.

'Pooh!' said Roland scornfully. 'What's the use of those to me? I am richer than everyone in the world put together.'

'Then look round my humble dwelling and choose what takes your fancy,' said the wizard at once. 'See, I have strange things here – what would you like?'

Roland glanced round quickly and saw the blue

milk jug, the silver spoon and the porridge plate on a shelf.

'Hm!' he said. 'I don't see much that I like. Wait! Here is a pretty jug. I will take that in return for the secret of the wind. And here is a dainty silver spoon. That shall be my reward for the secret of the rain. Then what shall I take for the secret of the thunder and lightning? Ah, here is a porridge plate I shall love to use. Wizard, I will take all these. Now see – here is an envelope. Inside you will find written the secret of the wind, the rain and the thunderstorm you have seen here tonight. Do not open it until tomorrow morning.'

He took the jug, the spoon and the porridge dish, and strode out of the door, the wizard bowing respectfully in front of him. Rosalind and Goldilocks had already climbed down the ladder and were waiting for him. They ran as fast as they could with all their watering cans, bellows and other things, laughing till they cried when they thought of the clever tricks they had played.

And when the king and queen heard of their prank they didn't know whether to scold or praise.

'You naughty, grave, rascally, daring scamps!' cried the queen. 'Why, you might have been turned into frogs!'

As for the wizard, when he opened the envelope the next morning and saw what was written there, he was very puzzled indeed. For this is what Roland had written: 'The secret of the wind is bellows. The secret of the rain is watering cans. The secret of the thunderstorm is fireworks. Ha! Ha!'

And now the poor wizard is wandering all over the world trying to find someone wise and clever enough to tell him the meaning of the bellows, the watering cans and the fireworks. But nobody likes to!

Mr Meddle Goes
Out Shopping

Mr Meddle Goes Out Shopping

WHEN MEDDLE was staying with a friend in Heyho Village, he met all the people there and liked them very much. They didn't know his meddling ways, and they liked him too. So Meddle felt very happy indeed.

If only I could help them and show them what a clever, kindly chap I am! thought Meddle. *At home nobody trusts me, and they all laugh at me. It's too bad.*

Well, his chance came very soon. It happened that Mrs Tilly, Mrs Binks and Miss Tub all wanted to go for a morning's outing together, and they couldn't.

'What should I do with my baby if I went out for the morning?' sighed Mrs Tilly.

'And who would do my shopping?' said Mrs Binks.

'And who would take my dog for a walk?' said Miss Tub, who loved her little white dog very much.

Meddle was passing by, and he heard them talking. At once he swept off his hat, bowed low and said, 'Dear ladies, let me help you. I can take the baby out in its pram, do Mrs Binks's shopping and take the dog for a walk all at the same time! Pray let me do this for you!'

'Oh, thank you,' said Mrs Tilly, beaming at Mr Meddle. 'It *would* be kind of you to help us.'

She didn't know that Meddle loved meddling and that things always went wrong with him. She led him to where her baby lay asleep in its pram. It was a pretty, golden-haired child with plump little hands.

'There's little Peterkin,' she said. 'Now, if you'll just keep an eye on him for me, he'll be all right.'

'And here's my shopping list,' said Mrs Binks, giving him a long list.

'Thank you,' said Meddle. He put the list into his

pocket. 'And now let me have your dog,' he said to Miss Tub.

Miss Tub gave him her dog's lead. 'His name is Spot,' she said. 'Do you see his big black spot? He is such a darling little dog.'

The dog growled at Meddle. Meddle took the lead and thought that the dog didn't sound a darling at all.

'Well, thank you, dear Mr Meddle,' said the three women, and they nodded at him and then went off for their morning's outing.

Meddle felt very proud. What a lot of help he was giving, to be sure!

'I'll walk down to the village now,' he said to himself. 'I can wheel the pram and hold the dog's lead in my hand to make the dog come along too – and I will go to the grocer's and get all the things that Mrs Binks wants.'

So off he went, wheeling the pram and dragging along the dog, who didn't seem to want to come a bit! Soon he met his friend, Mr Giggle, who stared in amazement.

'Whatever are you doing, Meddle?' he said. 'Where did you get that baby from – and the dog?'

'I'm helping people a bit, Giggle,' said Meddle. 'I'll be in to dinner all right. I've just promised to mind this baby and this dog and do a spot of shopping.'

Giggle began to laugh. Meddle looked offended and walked off, pushing the pram and dragging the dog. Soon he came to the grocer's shop. He went inside, first putting the pram against the shop window and tying the dog to a post. He pulled a list from his pocket.

Silly old Meddle! It wasn't Mrs Binks's list at all! It was a list he had made out for himself three weeks before – but Meddle didn't think of that. He thought it was the right one, of course.

He ordered all the things on the list. They were what he had ordered just before he gave a party. 'One pound of chocolate biscuits,' said Meddle. 'Two pounds of best butter. A two-pound pot of strawberry jam. One pound of shortbread and two bottles of lemonade.'

That was all there was on the list. Meddle looked at it, feeling a little surprised. 'I thought it was a longer list,' he said. 'I must have been wrong about that.'

The grocer put all the things into Meddle's net bag. Outside went Meddle, and walked to the first pram he saw. It wasn't Mrs Tilly's pram at all, nor her baby either! Somebody else had put their pram outside the shop since Meddle had put his, but dear old Meddle didn't think of that! He didn't even look at the baby inside. If he had, he would have seen that it was a dark-haired little girl, not a golden-haired baby boy!

Meddle hung his bag on the pram handle, put off the brake on the pram and started for home. He hadn't gone very far when he remembered the dog! He had left it behind.

'Bother!' said Meddle. 'Oh, bother! Now I must go back to fetch it!'

So back he went, pushing the pram. 'Let me see,

what was that dog like?' wondered Meddle, trying to remember. 'Oh yes – it was called Spot. It has a spot on its coat.'

He walked back to the grocer's, and when he was nearly there a large dog met him. 'Hallo!' said Meddle, staring at him. 'You've got a spot on your tail. You must be Spot!'

The dog wagged his tail. His name *was* Spot. Most dogs with spots on their back seem to be called Spot, and this dog was a very friendly one, willing to go to anyone who said his name.

'So you *are* Spot!' said Meddle. 'Where's your lead, you bad dog?'

'Woof, woof!' said the dog, gambolling round Meddle.

'You've lost that lead of yours, Spot,' said Meddle sternly. 'What do you suppose Miss Tub will say to you?'

'Woof, woof!' said the dog again, not knowing at all who Miss Tub was.

'Come here, sir,' said Meddle, and he caught the dog by the collar. He slipped a string through it and tied the dog to the pram handle. Then off he went again. He took the baby for a long walk, and then went back to Mrs Tilly's garden to wait for her to return.

He sat there, reading, very pleased with himself. If only the people in his own village could see how folk here trusted him with their babies and dogs and shopping! Ha, they would be sorry they had ever laughed at him.

At twenty minutes to one Mrs Tilly, Mrs Binks and Miss Tub came back. They went into the garden and smiled at Meddle, who jumped up at once and bowed politely.

Mrs Tilly looked at the pram and gave a jump. She went very red and stared at Meddle.

'Where's my baby?' she said.

'In the pram, of course, sweet little thing!' said Meddle, gazing fondly at the sleeping baby. He was a little astonished to see a dark-haired one – surely the other had been golden-haired?

'Meddle, this is *not* my baby!' said Mrs Tilly, looking like a fierce mother cat all of a sudden. 'And this is not my pram either, though it is dark blue like mine. WHAT HAVE YOU DONE WITH MY BABY?'

She looked so very fierce that Meddle was frightened. He took a step backwards and fell over the dog. The dog growled.

'Be quiet, Spot,' said Meddle. 'How dare you trip me up!'

'*That's* not Spot,' said Miss Tub. 'My dog is little and white with a black spot. This one is large and black with a white spot! WHAT HAVE YOU DONE WITH MY DOG?'

'Not your dog?' said Meddle, looking at the dog in surprise. 'Well, but he must be. How could a dog change like that? And how could a baby change either? You must have forgotten what your baby looked like,

Mrs Tilly, and you must have forgotten your dog, Miss Tub.'

'And what about my shopping?' said Mrs Binks, looking at the net bag. 'Do you suppose that is what was on my list, Meddle?'

'Certainly,' said Meddle, opening the bag. 'Biscuits, lemonade, shortbread, butter . . .'

'I didn't put *any* of those on my list!' said Mrs Binks angrily. 'This is just a horrid joke you are playing on us, Meddle. Well, I won't pay you for those things – you can pay for them yourself and take them home!'

Just then there was a scraping at the front gate and in came the right Spot, dragging his lead behind him! He had managed to get free! Miss Tub ran to him and hugged him.

'So here you are!' she said. 'Did that wicked Meddle leave you behind, poor darling! You can bite him if you like, the horrid fellow!'

'Grrrrrrrrr!' said Spot, showing his teeth at poor Meddle. Meddle made up his mind to go – if only he

45

could slip out without being noticed! But Spot wouldn't let him go. He stood by the gate, growling!

Suddenly someone came hurrying down the road with a dark-blue pram. She saw Mrs Tilly and called to her. 'Mrs Tilly! I've lost my baby! I found yours alone outside the grocer's shop, and I wondered if someone had taken mine instead. So I've brought yours for you – have you got mine?'

'Oh yes, I have!' cried Mrs Tilly joyfully. She rushed to her baby and took it out of its pram, talking lovingly to it. Meddle thought it would be a good time to get out of the gate.

But just as he was going, Spot rushed at him and bit a big hole in his trousers! Mrs Binks picked a tomato from a nearby plant and threw it at him – splosh! – and Mrs Tilly called out that she would get a policeman because he had stolen someone else's baby!

Poor Meddle! He ran back to Mr Giggle's in a hurry. He fetched his bag. He wouldn't even stop to eat his dinner. He caught the first bus home – and went into his house with the biscuits, shortbread, lemonade, jam and butter.

'I'm a most unlucky fellow,' he said sadly, as he spread butter on the biscuits and poured out some lemonade. 'A most unlucky fellow!'

The Squirrels and the Nuts

The Squirrels and the Nuts

THERE WERE once two red squirrels who lived in Windy Woods.

When the autumn came and nuts hung on the hazel trees the two feasted merrily. They went to the beech trees too, and picked out the kernels of the beech nuts. What a fine time they had!

Then a cold, bitter wind began to blow through Windy Woods, and although the squirrels wrapped themselves up well in their bushy tails, they could not keep themselves warm.

'Let us go to our nests and sleep while the cold weather lasts,' said one squirrel.

'First we must hide some nuts,' said the other. 'We shall be hungry when we wake up.'

So one squirrel hid his nuts in the crack of a tree, and the other hid his under a pile of dead leaves. Then they each went to their nests, curled themselves up and fell fast asleep.

Now when February came, the sun shone out warmly for two or three days, and the primroses began to peep in Windy Woods. The two squirrels woke up and stretched themselves. Cold weather might come again – but they were not going to sleep through this warm spell! No – they wanted a game and a meal! Out they frisked and said good morning to one another. Then they began to hunt for their nuts. They soon found them, just where they had hidden them – in the crack of a tree, and under the pile of dead leaves in the ditch. But then they began to quarrel about whose nuts were which.

'I tell you *I* put my nuts in this tree!' chattered one squirrel, 'and *you* put your nuts under the leaves! Mine are bigger and better than yours!'

'You storyteller!' cried the second squirrel. 'I know quite well that the nuts in the ditch are yours – all the rest are mine! You are greedy – you want the best, that's what it is!'

'Take that!' cried the first squirrel in anger, and struck the other a blow on the nose. Then they began to fight, crying, 'The nuts in the tree are mine! The ones in the ditch are yours!'

They made such a noise that two wood mice, a dormouse and a nuthatch bird came to see what was the matter. A hedgehog came too – but after a few minutes only the hedgehog was to be seen watching. The others had gone. The squirrels fought till they had no breath left, and had pulled out a great deal of their pretty coats. Then they sat and panted.

'Let us *share* all the nuts,' said the first one. 'Then we shall each have the same.'

So they ran to get the nuts – but to their great surprise, not a single one was there! None was in the tree or in the ditch either! Not one!

'Have *you* taken them?' they shouted to the watching hedgehog.

'I!' said the hedgehog in scorn. 'I never eat nuts! I like beetles and grubs. Ask the two wood mice, the dormouse and the nuthatch bird, not me! People who lose their temper lose other things too!'

Off he went – and in their homes the two wood mice and the dormouse chuckled as they gnawed at the nuts – and the nuthatch laughed too, as he wedged a hazelnut into the bark of a tree and split open the shell with his hard beak. Only the two squirrels didn't laugh. they looked at one another and nodded their pretty heads. 'Yes, yes,' they said sorrowfully, 'it's true – people who lose their tempers lose other things too!'

Peeko's Prank

Peeko's Prank

LITTLE PRINCE Peeko was the despair of his nurse, his tutor and his parents. He was the jolliest, merriest little chap, but, dear me! Nobody could keep him clean for two minutes together, and although his clothes were made by the best tailors in the land they always looked a perfect disgrace before Peeko had worn them half an hour.

You see, he loved making mud pies, splashing through puddles, sitting on the wet grass, squeezing through blackberry bushes and playing with such exciting things as soot, flour, treacle or water.

'He doesn't do any of the things a prince ought to

do,' sighed his nurse.

'He does everything he shouldn't!' growled his tutor.

'What *can* we do with him?' wondered his parents.

Prince Peeko wished people wouldn't bother about him so much.

'If only I could wear an overall, a pair of wings and nothing else, like all the other boy and girl fairies!' he sighed. 'I'm tired of long-pointed shoes that I'm always tumbling over, and tired of beautiful suits, and very tired of fine caps that somehow *always* blow off into a puddle!'

'Princes oughtn't to *want* to go and play in the mud with other dirty little boy fairies as *you* do!' scolded his nurse. 'You ought to sit properly with your book, and learn to keep yourself clean and princely. Now, just you come here and let me wash you and dress you in your fine new suit, ready to meet the Lord High Chamberlains of Dreamland and Fairy Town. They are paying a visit this afternoon to their Majesties, your father and mother.'

'Oh, tails and whiskers!' sighed the prince. 'What a nuisance!'

'Whoever taught you to use such vulgar expressions as "tails and whiskers"?' asked his nurse in horror.

'It isn't vulgar,' said the prince. 'One of my best friends, the sandy rabbit who lives in the woods, says it.'

'Dear, dear, dear, to think you go and play with people like that!' sighed his nurse, buttoning up the prince in a brand-new tunic.

'Tails and whiskers, it *is* tight!' groaned Peeko, twisting and wriggling.

When he was dressed the prince was taken up to the great meeting hall of the palace, and there he sat down on a grand golden chair by his father and mother, the king and queen. The chair was too high for him and terribly hard, and Peeko didn't like it a bit. His new suit was so tight that he really thought he would burst.

Just then he caught sight of the two visitors

coming in heralded by grand trumpeters with a fanfare of trumpets.

Up stepped the two Lord High Chamberlains to greet the king and queen and the little prince.

Peeko stared at them in surprise, for they were wearing things he had never seen before – fine frilly, starched ruffs sticking up all round their necks.

It makes them look as if they're serving their heads up on a white dinner plate! thought Peeko. *I suppose it's a new fashion. What a funny thing fashion is, to be sure! How uncomfortable they must be with pointed shoes to fall over, tight suits to squash them and those funny stick-out collars to choke them!*

Everyone at court thought the two visitors were most grand. No one had ever seen ruffs before, and all were trying to get a good view of the fashionable chamberlains, and making up their minds to tell their dressmakers and tailors to make them ruffs as soon as possible.

As Peeko listened to the long speeches that the

king, his lords and the two visitors made, he became very much bored. Then suddenly he felt a sneeze coming!

Oh, dear, oh, dear! How dreadful to sneeze in such grand, polite company! Poor Peeko tried his hardest to stop it, but the sneeze *would* come!

A-TISHOO-SHOO-SHOO! sneezed Peeko very loudly indeed.

And three of the buttons on his little tight suit burst off, and flew straight at the nose of the surprised Lord High Chamberlain.

'I'm sorry!' cried Peeko, very much upset. 'But I *told* Mother I should burst my suit!'

'Sh! Sh!' said everyone around, and Peeko was hustled off by his tutor at once.

'Such shocking behaviour!' said Sir Griffles, his tutor. 'Sneezing and bursting like that!'

Everyone seemed most shocked at the prince's behaviour, and the king and queen were very much distressed.

'It must be because he plays with the fairies and animals outside the palace!' said the queen. 'We shall have to be stricter with him, and *make* him keep clean and wear his clothes properly, and learn nice manners. Oh, and I mustn't forget, Nurse. Everyone is going to be in the new fashion and wear ruffs round their necks now. So see that Prince Peeko has a nice one, won't you.'

'Yes, Your Majesty,' said the nurse. 'But, dear me, how he will grumble, to be sure!'

And so he did. It was bad enough to wear tight suits, but as for a ruff as well!

'I *can't* wear it,' cried Peeko. 'I can't, I can't! I hate my long shoes that I tumble over, and I *hate* tight suits, and now to expect me to wear ruffs! No, Nurse, I can't.'

But he had to, and no boy fairy in the kingdom felt so miserable. The ruff rubbed his chin and hurt his neck, and made him feel as if he really couldn't breathe. All the rest of the court wore ruffs too, but *they* seemed to like them very much. Peeko really couldn't understand it.

He was very unhappy, for he was closely watched, and was not allowed to go and play with any other fairy or animal. But at last one day he escaped from his tutor and ran into the fields. There he sat down and sighed very deeply.

'Hallo!' said the sandy rabbit, lolloping up. 'What's the matter?'

'Yes, what's the matter?' cried the little fairies, flying up astonished to see their merry playmate so downcast.

'I lead an awful life nowadays,' said Prince Peeko sadly. 'Look at the clothes I have to wear – and look at this terrible choking ruff that everyone's wearing now.'

The fairies were sorry for Peeko, for they loved him.

'Why don't you get rid of all the ruffs?' asked one of them. 'Then if nobody could wear them, the fashion would go out, and *you* wouldn't have to wear one either.'

'How could they be got rid of?' asked Peeko.

'If you can manage to get the ruffs,' said the sandy rabbit, 'we'll hide them away so that no one can find them!'

So that night Peeko stole into all the bedrooms of the palace, picked up the ruffs, popped them into a bag and gave them to the sandy rabbit out of the window. Then he went to bed.

Well, next morning there was such a to-do! No one could find his ruff, and everyone came down to breakfast with their necks free and uncovered, including Peeko.

'Who has done this thing?' thundered the king angrily.

'I have,' said Peeko bravely. 'Don't look so cross, Father. I'm tired of being in the fashion, and so all the ruffs have been hidden. I'll promise to give you back yours and everyone else's if only you'll let me off wearing mine.'

'Certainly not,' said the king, astonished. 'My servants will soon find the ruffs, and you shall be punished, Peeko, for your naughtiness!'

Well, Peeko was punished but no one could find the frilly ruffs *any*where! The king was most surprised – and to his astonishment he found he was very glad.

'It's nice to have a day without feeling choked!' he found himself thinking. 'I wish I could wear a suit that wasn't so tight too!'

Then he began thinking hard – and before very long he had decided that Peeko was the most sensible person in the palace.

After all, why should we choke and squash ourselves! he thought. *I'll straight away make a new fashion!*

And so he did. He sent his heralds round to say that henceforth ruffs were out of fashion, suits were to be loose and shoes need not be pointed.

He sent for Peeko, scolded him, kissed him and

then gave him – what do you think – an overall made of a poppy petal.

'There you are,' he said. 'That's your suit in future. Now go away and be good. And tell me, Peeko – where *have* those ruffs been hidden?'

Peeko told him, and I'll tell you so that you can go and find them this month. The sandy rabbit and the fairies poked them tightly underneath the heads of all the mushrooms and toadstools they could find! And there you'll see them if you look – lovely little frills neatly hidden under the cap of every creamy pink mushroom and every yellow-brown toadstool!

The Story That Came True

The Story That Came True

WILFRID WASN'T a very nice little boy. He liked to frighten children smaller than himself and he told a lot of stories. Then suddenly one of his stories came true, and he didn't like it at all! I'll tell you about it.

Wilfrid went to boarding school. It was a nice school, and had the biggest, loveliest garden for playing in that you can imagine. Down at the very bottom was a dell with old trees. One of them was hollow.

Wilfrid liked this dell, and he especially liked the hollow tree. He kept all his treasures in it, and when his mother sent him sweets and fruit he didn't share them with the others, he hid them in the tree.

This dell shall be mine, he thought to himself. *And that hollow tree shall be mine. Nobody else must come here.*

And so he began to tell horrid stories about the dell.

'I've seen a fox there,' he told the surprised children in his class. 'A nasty, slinky fox that looked as if it would bite like anything. Don't you go near that dell!'

The other children didn't like the sound of the fox at all, and they kept away from the dell. All except little Geoffrey, who wasn't afraid of foxes at all, because his aunt had once looked after a fox cub and he had loved it.

So he went down to the dell to find the fox. He wandered around but, of course, he saw no fox. Wilfrid saw him there and was very angry. Then he remembered that Geoffrey wasn't afraid of foxes. He ran up to him and pushed him away so suddenly that Geoffrey was startled.

'Geoff! Quick, come away! There's a wolf here!' said Wilfrid, pretending to be frightened. 'He must have chased the fox away! Run, quickly!'

'There isn't a wolf!' said Geoffrey, staring all round. 'I've been everywhere in the dell and I've not seen one.'

'Look – he's in that hollow tree – he's peeping out at us!' cried Wilfrid. 'That's his home.'

Well, somehow Geoffrey didn't like the sound of that at all, and he turned and ran. Wilfrid was very pleased. Aha! Now Geoffrey would tell everyone there was a wolf living in that hollow tree, and nobody would know where he had hidden his tin of biscuits.

The wolf story went on for quite a long time. Wilfrid kept saying how he had gone to watch for the wolf, and had seen him in the dell, sometimes sharpening his claws on one of the trees, sometimes peeping from behind a bush, watching for someone to come, and sometimes fast asleep in the hollow tree.

At half-term a new little girl came to the small boarding school. She was bright-eyed and jolly and everyone liked her. How she stared when the others told her not to go near the dell because of the wolf.

'But there aren't any wolves in this country,' she

said. 'You know there aren't! Who made up that silly story?'

'Wilfrid told us,' said Geoffrey. 'First there was a fox there, and then a wolf came and chased the fox away, and now the wolf is there always. He lives in a hollow tree there.'

'I don't believe it,' said Nora, the new little girl. 'I shall tell Wilfrid so.'

So she did. 'I don't believe in your wolf,' she said to him. 'It's a silly untruth. You know wolves don't live in this country.'

'I know that,' said Wilfrid. 'This one may have escaped from the zoo. But, as a matter of fact, it's gone now. There's a bear there instead! A big brown bear. He's even fiercer than the wolf, so you'd better all be jolly careful to keep away from the dell.'

He stalked away, and the others stared after him. He always seemed so *certain* about these animals in the dell. Nora laughed.

She turned to the others. 'Listen to me,' she said.

'I'm going to play a lovely trick on Wilfrid, and you must all keep the secret.'

'Oh, what is it?' cried all the others.

'Well, my aunt lives in this town, and I'm going to see her tomorrow,' said Nora. 'And she's got a big furry coat in one of the rooms. I shall borrow it! I shall bring it here and hide it in a shed, covered with sacks. And the next day I shall take it to the dell, cover myself in it and make loud, grunting noises.'

The children squealed with delight. Nora jumped up and down in excitement.

'You must all go and tell Wilfrid there's something strange in the dell, that growls and grunts, and ask him if it is his bear,' said Nora. 'And he'll go to the dell, of course, and he'll see *me* – with the coat on! What a shock for him when he sees what he thinks is a *real* bear there! He will think his silly story has come true – and I don't somehow think he'll make up any more!'

The children were so excited over their secret that

they could hardly keep quiet about it. Nora was as good as her word. She went to see her aunt the next day, and managed to slip back to the school in the evening with the big fur coat over her shoulder. She took it to the shed and covered it with sacks. It was a fine coat, and the hood was enormous.

'It's lovely and furry,' said Nora, covering up the coat.

Next day Nora dragged the coat to the dell. Geoffrey helped to put it over her. Then down she went behind the hollow tree, on all fours, the big hood hiding her own completely. She began to grunt loudly.

Geoffrey laughed. 'Lovely! Awfully real!' he said in delight. 'I'm off to tell Wilfrid now. I'll get the other children and post them all round the dell to enjoy the fun.'

He sped off, telling the others on the way. They laughed and went with him to Wilfrid, pretending to look scared and alarmed.

'Wilfrid,' said Geoffrey in a scared voice. 'You

know that bear you say is in the dell – the one that lives in the hollow tree?'

'Yes,' said Wilfrid.

'Well – it's grunting awfully loudly today,' said Geoffrey. 'You come and hear it.'

'It's probably cross because somebody went near the dell,' said Wilfrid, and went off with the others, Geoffrey leading the way.

When they got near the dell they could all hear the grunting. Nora was doing it very well indeed. Geoffrey badly wanted to laugh, but he didn't.

Wilfrid looked surprised. Certainly there *was* a grunting noise in the dell. How strange! He knew it couldn't really be the bear he had talked about, because it was only a pretend bear that he had made up. Still – what was that grunting noise?

He went boldly into the dell – and at the same moment Nora lumbered out from behind the hollow tree, doing louder grunts than ever!

The children had been told to squeal when they saw

her, and squeal they did. But Wilfrid didn't squeal. No, he went very pale indeed and stared at the bear as if he couldn't believe his eyes. He had made up a story about a bear to frighten the others – and here, before his eyes, *was* a bear!

The others ran away, as they had been told. All except Geoffrey, who stood watching Wilfrid. The bear came a little nearer and began to growl very deeply. Geoffrey thought how well Nora did it. Wilfrid gave a loud squeal of fright and turned to run. But he was so very scared that his feet seemed glued to the ground. He couldn't move!

'Wilfrid – come quickly!' said Geoffrey, trying not to burst into laughter. He tugged at his arm. 'Come along – the bear's coming for you! You always said there was one, and here it is! Run.'

And at last poor Wilfrid ran. His legs could hardly carry him, and when he got to the seat outside the school he fell on it, looking quite green.

The others clustered round. Geoffrey spoke to

them. 'It's quite a nice bear, really,' he said. 'I shan't be at all afraid of it. I shall go and play in the dell whenever I like.'

'So shall we!' said the others. But Wilfrid turned even greener.

'I shan't,' he said. 'I shall never, never go near the dell again!'

And he didn't. He couldn't understand how the others dared to. They found his hidey-hole in the hollow tree and pulled out his tin of biscuits and his bottle of sweets.

'There – look at those,' said Nora in disgust. 'He put them there so that he didn't need to share them with us. He made up his silly tales to frighten us and keep us away from his precious biscuits and things. He's a horrid boy and he deserves his fright. And nobody is ever to tell him that the bear he saw wasn't a real one. Let him think it's one of his wicked stories come true – he won't tell any again in a hurry!'

Well, he didn't. Poor Wilfrid had frightened other

children very often – now he had had a real fright himself, and he knew what it was like. No more stories for him! Just suppose they all came true, like the one about the bear!

The Bad Cockyolly
Bird

The Bad Cockyolly Bird

THE COCKYOLLY bird lived in the nursery with the other toys. He was a colourful creature, with red plush wings, a yellow tail and a green body. He could be wound up, and then he walked along in a jerky manner, saying 'Kack, kack, kack!' as he went.

Now the Cockyolly bird was a great nuisance. He was always picking up things that belonged to other people, and running off with them.

He ran off with the big doll's hair ribbon, and she couldn't find it anywhere. Where do you suppose he had put it? He had stuffed it up the tap in the basin. When Nurse turned on the tap, out came the ribbon! She was so surprised.

He ran off with the baby doll's shoes. The baby doll had taken them off because they were rather tight, and she was enjoying herself, running about in her bare feet. And when she wanted her shoes they had gone.

'The Cockyolly bird took them,' said the clockwork mouse. 'I saw him. He has thrown them out of the window!'

So the baby doll had to climb down the apple tree outside and go to hunt for her slippers in the dark. She didn't like it at all.

Everyone scolded the Cockyolly bird, but he only grinned and said, 'Kack! If I could find some place to put your things so that you wouldn't find them so easily, I'd hide them away properly.'

And then one day the Cockyolly bird *did* find a place to put things – where do you suppose it was? You'll never guess! It was in the big moneybox that stood up on the nursery mantelpiece.

He found a button off the soldier's tunic and he picked it up and popped it into the slit of the moneybox. Clink! It fell in among the pennies and lay there. Then the Cockyolly bird hunted about for something else and found the lamb's tail. It was always loose and had fallen off on to the floor.

The Cockyolly bird picked it up and flew off with it. He stuffed it into the moneybox. Aha! The lamb wouldn't know where it had gone. He would look for it all over the place.

Then the Cockyolly bird found the brooch belonging to the walking doll. Dear me, he *was* pleased! He had once asked the walking doll to lend it to him when he went to a party, and she wouldn't – so now she would be punished, thought the bad Cockyolly bird! He pushed it into the moneybox. It fell inside with a little tinkling noise.

But the worst thing he did was to take the teddy bear's glass eye. The bear had two beautiful eyes, both made of brown glass, round and shining. But one was loose and sometimes came out. Then it had to be stuck in again.

The teddy bear wanted to romp about one night, so he took his loose eye out and laid it carefully down on a chair in the doll's house. That was where the Cockyolly bird found it. He picked it up in his beak and flew off with it at once. Clink! It went into the moneybox.

Oh, what a to-do there was when the teddy bear found his eye gone! 'I know that wicked Cockyolly bird has taken it,' he cried. 'Oh, I know he has!'

The toys surrounded the Cockyolly bird and shouted at him:

'Where's the teddy bear's eye?'

'Where's the walking doll's brooch?'

'Where's the lamb's tail?'

'Where's the soldier's button?'

'Aha! Oho! Where *you* won't be able to get them,' grinned the Cockyolly bird. 'They are all in the moneybox.'

The toys stared at one another in dismay. In the

moneybox! Why, that was always locked – they would never be able to get anything out of that.

'Oh, you bad, wicked Cockyolly bird!' shouted everyone in a rage. The Cockyolly bird flung back his head and laughed and laughed and laughed. He did like to see the toys so angry. As he laughed, his key came loose, and suddenly it dropped to the floor. Clang!

In a trice the baby doll caught it up in her hand. She raced to the nearest chair. She climbed up it, all the way to the back. She jumped from there to the mantelpiece – and she ran to the moneybox. She dropped the Cockyolly bird's key into the slit in the moneybox. Clang!

Everyone stared. The Cockyolly bird broke into loud wailing.

'Kack! Kack! What have you done with my key? When I am run down I shan't be able to be wound up. I shan't be able to walk, or fly, or peck. Oh, you wicked baby doll!'

'You deserve it,' said everyone at once. 'If you put things belonging to *us* in the moneybox, why shouldn't we put in things belonging to *you*! It serves you right!'

So it did. When his clockwork ran down, there was no key to wind up the Cockyolly bird, so he just had to stand in his corner and glare at everyone, and wish and wish that he had never been so foolish as to tell people what a good hiding place the moneybox was!

When Mother's birthday came the children who lived in the nursery opened their moneybox to get out some money to buy Mother a present, and dear me, *how* surprised they were to find so many strange things inside.

'How did they get there?' they said to one another. But nobody knew.

The Cockyolly bird got his key back. The teddy bear got his glass eye back, and all the others got their things back too.

'And just remember this, Cockyolly bird,' said the teddy bear, as he stuck in his glass eye once more and glared at the bird with it, 'we shall only be too pleased to put your key in the moneybox if you play any more tricks. So behave yourself in future.'

And now the Cockyolly bird is as good as gold. He did get such a shock when his key went into the moneybox – he doesn't want it to happen again, you may be sure!

Mother Minky's Trick

Mother Minky's Trick

MOTHER MINKY was a very good cook. She made pies and cakes, tarts and buns, and they were really most delicious.

She had a very broad windowsill, and she always put her goodies there to cool. She kept a sharp eye for the birds, who would dearly have loved to peck a bit out of a pie. Her cat, Snoozer, always lay below the window, to help Mother Minky to guard her baking.

Now one morning Mother Minky made four meat pies, two apple pies, six cherry buns and two currant cakes. They were all as perfect as could be. The old dame put them out on the windowsill and called to Snoozer the cat.

'Snoozer! Wake up for a while! There are plenty of things for you to guard this morning! Don't you let those greedy starlings come and steal, will you?'

'Mee-ow,' answered Snoozer, stretching himself and winking his yellow eyes at his mistress.

He lay and watched carefully. The birds saw his yellow eyes glinting, and they kept away. But when Mother Minky came to take in her baking, she gave a cry of surprise.

'Snoozer! There is a meat pie missing – and a currant cake! Now what has happened to them?'

Snoozer sat up in astonishment. He knew quite well that no bird had been down to the sill – and how could anyone else have taken the things? He would have seen them!

'You've been asleep, Snoozer,' said Mother Minky crossly. 'That is very bad of you. You will have no dinner!'

'Mee-ow-ow-ow,' said Snoozer sadly. He knew that he had not been asleep – but however could that pie and cake have gone?

Now the next morning Mother Minky put out three jam tarts to cool, and two chocolate cakes. She called to Snoozer.

'Snoozer! Sit up and watch, please. My cakes and tarts are cooling on the sill!'

Snoozer sat up straight. He cocked his sharp ears and opened his yellow eyes wide. He watched and watched, putting his claws in and out, ready to leap at any bird that flew down.

But no bird came – and yet when Mother Minky came to take in her goodies, there was only one tart and one cake on the sill. The others had gone!

She was very angry indeed. She scolded poor Snoozer and told him he was a very naughty cat, and she couldn't trust him any more. Snoozer waved his long tail about and felt dreadful. He knew quite well that he hadn't seen anyone taking those cakes – so how could they have gone?

Now the next time that Mother Minky put out her cakes, she watched them herself. And she saw a very strange and peculiar thing!

Snoozer was down below, watching in the garden. The cakes – four ginger ones and one large nut cake – were cooling on the sill. Mother Minky saw them quite clearly and then, all of a sudden, two ginger cakes leapt into the air and the nut cake followed! They flew off round the garden, through the gate and then were out of sight.

'Well!' said Mother Minky, most astonished. Her knees suddenly felt very weak, and she sat down on a chair. 'Never have I seen cakes do that before! Where have they gone? Why did they go?'

Quickly she then leant out of the window. 'Snoozer,' she called, 'did you smell or hear anything just then?'

'No-ee-oh,' answered Snoozer.

Mother Minky sat down again and thought. The cakes had flown off the windowsill, gone round the garden – *and gone out of the gate!* Now why should cakes go out of a gate? They didn't need to! They could quite well have flown over the hedge. Cakes didn't *need* to go out of gates, as people did.

'I think I know the answer to this riddle,' said Mother Minky at last. 'Yes, I think I know! The cakes didn't fly off by themselves – they were carried by somebody who couldn't be seen! He crept quietly to the window – lifted up the cakes – and then ran round the garden and through the gate. He must have been wearing a magic cap or cloak to make him unseen – the horrid little thief! Now I wonder who it is! I just wonder.'

But Mother Minky didn't know. 'I mean to find out though,' she said. 'Now what shall I do?'

She thought and thought. Then she rubbed her hands and smiled. Yes – she would use her blue-nose spell. She had had it for a long time and had never used it. Now it would be just the very thing!

So the next morning, when she made two big jam

tarts, she mixed the powdery blue-nose spell in with her flour. It was a curious blue colour, but it didn't show when the jam tarts were baked. Mother Minky put the tarts on the sill as usual.

In half an hour's time those two tarts seemed to jump off the sill, fly round the garden and go out of the gate. Mother Minky smiled. 'All right!' she said. 'You've gone, jam tarts – but I'll soon know who's taken you!'

That afternoon Mother Minky sent out a message to say that she was giving a party and please would everyone come to it. She would have it in the garden and give everybody a good time. She set to work to make dozens of cakes and buns.

Everybody was pleased. They loved Mother Minky's parties because her cakes were so delicious. They put on party dresses and went to Mother Minky's at four o'clock. Mother Minky looked quickly round at her guests – yes, everybody was there!

'The blue-nose spell will begin to work soon,' she said to herself. 'Ha, ha! The thief didn't know that there was a spell in those tarts that would turn his nose bright blue in six hours' time!'

The guests drank their tea and ate their buns. And then somebody pointed to a small pixie and began to laugh.

'Look! Look! Smarty has got a bright-blue nose. Smarty, what have you done to your nose?'

Smarty was astonished. He was a mean little pixie. He looked at his nose in a glass. Good gracious! It was as blue as the sky! What could have happened?

'I don't like it,' said Smarty, frightened. 'I think I'll go home. I don't know why my nose has gone blue.'

'But *I* do!' said Mother Minky in a sharp, angry voice. 'Come here, Smarty, and I will tell you.'

The pixie came near. Everyone crowded round and listened. '*Some*body has been stealing my cakes, pies and tarts each day,' began Mother Minky.

Smarty went pale. 'It wasn't me – it wasn't, it wasn't!' he cried.

'Be quiet,' said Mother Minky. 'Well, this morning

I thought I would catch the thief – so I put a blue-nose spell into my tarts. Whoever ate those tarts would have a blue nose six hours later. And *you*, Smarty, have a bright-blue nose!'

Well, Smarty was very frightened when he saw how angry everyone was looking. He knew he was in for a very good scolding! Quick as lightning he put on a little red cap – it was magic and made him vanish at once!

'Now you can't see me and I can escape!' shouted the bad little pixie. But he had forgotten his blue nose! It was strong blue magic, and although all the rest of him had vanished, his blue nose still shone like a little blue stone in the air. So everyone knew where he was!

That naughty pixie was well scolded before he managed to get to the gate and run out.

'You'll keep that blue nose just as long as you steal things, Smarty – so hurry up and turn over a new leaf!' called Mother Minky.

Smarty didn't stay in that village a day longer. He

was so ashamed. He packed up his things, put on his magic cap and, without being seen, ran off over the hills. But his blue nose could still be seen, and unless he has become honest, it is still wandering about the world like a little blue stone, about as high as your shoulder.

So if you see it, catch hold of it – and you'll have a pixie by the nose!

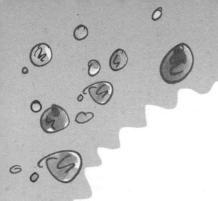

The Very Naughty Dog

The Very Naughty Dog

ONCE UPON a time there was a dog, and his name was Spot, because he had a black spot in the middle of his back. He had a master and a mistress, and he loved them both very much.

One day he saw that his mistress was very sad, and he heard what she said to the master.

'Oh, dear!' she said. 'I am so sorry to think we have got to leave this dear old house that we love so much. It makes me want to cry.'

'I am sorry too,' said the master. 'But you see we haven't enough money to pay our bills so we must leave here and go to a smaller house.'

'Will there be a garden for Spot to play in?' asked the mistress.

'Oh, no,' said the master. 'I don't even know if we shall be able to keep Spot. Perhaps we shall have to sell him.'

Well, it nearly broke Spot's heart to think of such a dreadful thing. So he went to tell his trouble to a great friend of his, an old brown horse that lived in a nearby field. The horse was very old and knew a lot of secrets. He was sorry to think that his friend Spot was going away, and he told him one of his secrets.

The next thing that happened was that Spot went to a bed of daffodils and jumped right in the middle of them. Then he began to dig them up!

The mistress saw him and called to him to stop. He didn't, so she went out and scolded him. But as soon as her back was turned he went to the bed and dug up the daffodils again and made a very big hole.

'You are a naughty dog,' said his mistress. 'You are a *very* naughty dog!' said his master, and took him by the collar. He was put into the corner in disgrace.

As soon as he was free again he went to the daffodil bed and dug a bigger hole than ever.

'You are a very, *very* naughty dog!' said his master and mistress together, and he was tied up. He gnawed and gnawed at his rope till he escaped. He went to the daffodil bed and dug such a very deep hole that he quite disappeared in it. And then he found what he wanted, just as his master and mistress came running up again.

'You very, very, *very* . . .' began his master, and then he stopped in surprise. For he saw something sticking out of the hole. And whatever do you think it was? Wuff, wuff, it was a great big chest full of gold money that his master's grandmother had hidden there years and years ago. That was the secret that the old brown horse had told him.

'Just look there!' cried his master, and he dragged the chest out and opened it. When he saw the money he was full of joy, and he and the mistress and

Spot jumped round the hole and shouted and barked in excitement.

'You good dog!' said the mistress. 'You *very* good dog!' said the master. And they kissed him and stroked him and patted him, and gave him two bones, three biscuits and a new ball. Then they all lived happily ever afterwards.

Tiddley-Pom the Tailor

Tiddley-Pom the Tailor

ONE DAY, Very-Small the Gnome was walking home along by Bumble Bee Common, when he came across Bo-Bo the Wizard looking very much upset.

'What's the matter, Bo-Bo?' asked Very-Small.

'I've lost my spectacles,' said Bo-Bo in a sad voice. 'I can't find them anywhere. I'm as blind as a bat without them too.'

'I'll help you to look for them,' said Very-Small. 'Perhaps you've dropped them in the long grass here.'

He looked and looked and looked, but nowhere could he see them. So he went back to Bo-Bo to tell him so. And then he suddenly saw them. They were pushed high up on Bo-Bo's forehead and he had forgotten that he had put them there!

Very-Small began to laugh. Then he pointed to the spectacles and said, 'Oh, Bo-Bo, your spectacles are up on your forehead. They are not lost at all!'

Bo-Bo was surprised and delighted to find them. He put up his hand and pulled them down on to his nose. Ah, now he was quite all right again – he could see perfectly well.

'It was very good of you to try to find them for me,' he said to the gnome. 'I'm sure I would never have guessed they were on my forehead all the time, if you hadn't seen them. I'll give you a little reward.'

He felt in his pocket and brought out a little green thing, rather like a marble, but small and soft.

'Here you are,' he said to Very-Small. 'It's all I have with me. You can have it.'

'What is it?' asked Very-Small.

'It's a skippetty-spell,' said Bo-Bo. 'Be careful how you use it.'

Well, Very-Small was always pleased to have any kind of spell, so he took it and said thank you. He ran off whistling, with the spell in his pocket.

Now he hadn't gone very far when he heard a curious noise and he looked into the ditch to see what had made it. Lying on his back there was Tiddley-Pom, the king's tailor, fast asleep. He had taken off his shoes and they stood beside him.

'My word, Tiddley-Pom will be late at the palace!' said Very-Small to himself. 'He's got to measure the king for a new suit at a quarter to three, because he told me so himself this morning. Shall I wake him?'

Very-Small was just going to shake Tiddley-Pom, when he saw the shoes – and a very naughty thought came into his head. He would put the skippetty-spell into them, and see what happened!

So he took it quickly out of his pocket and broke it in half. He put half in each shoe and then chuckled loudly. He went to hide behind a tree, and when he was safely there, he threw a fir cone at Tiddley-Pom, to wake him.

It hit him on the nose, and he awoke with a jump.

'What hit me?' said Tiddley-Pom sleepily, sitting up and rubbing his eyes. 'Was it a drop of rain? What's the time?'

He took out his watch and looked at it. Then he gave a shout of surprise.

'Jumping pigs! It's half past two! I shall never be at the palace in time!'

Quickly he put on his shoes and buttoned them tightly. Then he stood up.

Very-Small was watching behind the tree, wondering what was going to happen. He soon saw.

No sooner had Tiddley-Pom put on the shoes than the spell began to work. The tailor hadn't taken six steps before he felt something very funny about his feet. They began to tap the ground and to skip about. Tiddley-Pom didn't know what to make of it all.

Very-Small nearly burst his tight little coat with trying not to laugh out loud. He thought it was very funny to see old Tiddley-Pom dancing away by himself in the road like that, looking most astonished and alarmed.

He followed him without being seen. The poor tailor went hopping and skipping along the road, quite unable to understand why he was doing such funny things. He tried to keep his feet still, but he couldn't. They went on and on skipping and tripping.

'Well now, what can be the matter with my feet?' said Tiddley-Pom in a worried voice. 'Never before have I known them behave like this.'

He didn't know that it was his shoes which were causing all the trouble. He didn't know what to think about it at all. He was very anxious to get to the palace in time, and so he did his best to keep his feet turned in the right direction. Off they went, prancing and jumping like a pair of ponies. Very-Small thought he had never seen anything so funny in his life.

At last Tiddley-Pom arrived at the palace gates, and danced in past the astonished sentries, who wondered whatever was wrong with the king's tailor. He pranced his way into the throne room and tried to keep his feet still while he bowed before the king, but he couldn't.

The king stared at him in amazement. He had never seen Tiddley-Pom doing anything so extraordinary before, and he wondered if the tailor had had a sunstroke or something.

'What's the matter, Tiddley-Pom?' he asked. 'Keep still a moment, please – don't skip all over the place like that, it's most disturbing.'

'Oh, please, Your Majesty, I can't help it,' said poor Tiddley-Pom. 'My feet just won't stop. I never knew anything like it.'

'Nonsense!' said the king. 'Stop at once. You're making me feel quite giddy!'

But the tailor couldn't stop, no matter how hard he tried, and soon the tears came into his eyes and ran down his cheeks. He was very much alarmed, and he was dreadfully afraid that the king would have him sent to prison for disobedience.

Then who should come to pay a call upon the king but Bo-Bo the Wizard! He walked into the throne room and bowed to His Majesty – and then he turned to stare at Tiddley-Pom's antics.

'Is this a new jester, or a comic dancer you have?' he asked in surprise.

'No,' said the king. 'It's Tiddley-Pom, my tailor. He says he can't stop his feet from dancing and skipping like that.'

The wizard took off his glasses and polished them. Then he put them on again and looked closely at Bo-Bo's feet.

'There's nothing wrong with his feet,' he said. 'It's his shoes. It looks to me as if there's a skippetty-spell in them. Take off your shoes, Tiddley-Pom.'

With the greatest difficulty, the tailor bent down and took off his shoes, his feet jumping about all the time – but hey presto! As soon as the shoes were off, his feet stopped still, and Tiddley-Pom was himself again. He was so glad that he wept loudly into his handkerchief, while the king patted him on the back and told him not to mind.

'This is a funny thing,' said Bo-Bo, peering into the shoes and taking out two bits of green. 'This is the same spell that I gave to Very-Small not an hour ago. He must have put it into Tiddley-Pom's shoes. How very naughty of him!'

'Fetch him here,' said the king, frowning.

Two servants went to find Very-Small, and there he was at the gate of the palace, waiting to see the tailor come skipping out again. He was very much surprised to be led before the king, for he hadn't dreamt that his naughty trick would be found out.

'I am ashamed of you, Very-Small,' said the king. 'You ought to know better than this. You have made Tiddley-Pom very unhappy and worried, to say nothing of making him late to measure me for my new suit.'

'But he looked so funny,' said Very-Small, beginning to giggle.

'Perhaps you'd like to try the shoes yourself then,' said Bo-Bo, slipping the spell into them again and holding them out to Very-Small. 'I'm sure you'll find them funnier still when you've got them on. Give Tiddley-Pom your own shoes, and take his.'

Very-Small looked alarmed, but he had to obey. Tiddley-Pom put on the gnome's shoes, and Very-Small put on the skippetty-shoes. In a moment he was skipping and dancing all over the room!

How everyone laughed! How the king roared and Bo-Bo chuckled! As for Tiddley-Pom, he laughed so much that he burst a button off his coat.

Only Very-Small didn't laugh – he found that it wasn't funny at all. But he had to wear the skippetty-shoes for the rest of the day, and when at last he was allowed to take them off, he was so tired and so sorry for himself that I think it will be a very long time before he tries any more tricks of that sort again!

As for the spell, he threw it into the dustbin, and nobody has ever seen it since.

The Little Girl Who Told Stories

The Little Girl Who Told Stories

ONCE UPON a time there was a little girl called Rosaline. She was a pretty thing, with beautiful manners and a kind heart, but dear me, she told the most dreadful stories! She hardly ever kept to the truth, and her poor mother really didn't know how to cure her.

She would say that she had seen a parrot in the garden, when she had seen nothing but a little brown sparrow. She vowed that she was top girl in her class at school when really she was only fifth. She told her friends that she had twenty glorious frocks in her cupboard at home, when she had only four quite ordinary ones and one silk party frock.

So you can see what a dreadful little storyteller she was! It wasn't a bit of good Rosaline being kind and pretty, because she always spoilt everything by telling untruths.

One day she wandered into Wishing Wood, which was just near her home. She found a little path she had never seen before, and she ran down it, wondering where it went. After about half an hour she came to the funniest little house she had ever seen.

It was like a small hillock, about half as high again as Rosaline. Daisies grew thickly all over it, and it was a very pretty sight. In one side was a bright-yellow door with a blue knocker.

'Well!' said Rosaline, stopping in surprise. 'What a very peculiar little house! I wonder who lives in it?'

She very soon knew, for at that moment the yellow door flew open and a small man came out. He looked very much worried, and he beckoned to Rosaline.

'Can you cut thin sandwiches?' he asked.

Rosaline looked astonished. Then she nodded her head.

'Yes,' she said. 'I often cut them for Mummy when we're going picnicking.'

'Well, *do* come in and help me cut some,' begged the little man. 'I seem to be making such a mess of it.'

Rosaline followed him into the strange house. It was perfectly round inside, and the furniture was very small. On a little table was a big loaf of bread, a dish of butter and a jar of homemade potted meat.

'It's like this,' said the elf. 'I've been asked to a picnic today, and I promised to take some sandwiches. But I've never made any before, and so I can't seem to cut them nicely.'

Rosaline looked at the big pieces he had hacked off the loaf and tried to spread with butter.

'Yes, they are not very nice,' she said. 'Never mind, I'll do as many as you want.'

She asked him for a knife and then set to work.

She was neat and quick with her hands, and soon had a fine pile of thin, well-buttered sandwiches on a plate. When she had made twenty, the little man told her that was enough.

'They are beautifully made!' he said gratefully. 'Thank you so much. Now I should like to give you something in return for your kindness.'

'Oh, no, that's quite all right,' said Rosaline politely.

'It would please me very much to give you a nice present,' said the little man. 'Come with me, and you shall choose something for yourself.'

He lifted up a trapdoor in the floor, and Rosaline saw a flight of steps leading downwards. The elf led the way and she followed. They went along a dark passage lit dimly by an old hanging lantern, and then came to a big cave. In it were sitting many other little men, all hard at work.

'What are they doing?' whispered Rosaline.

'Look and see,' answered the little man.

She bent over the busy elves and saw that they

were making all kinds of marvellous jewellery. Green precious stones, blue ones, yellow, white and red, every colour was there, and each stone was being set into wonderful glittering necklaces, bracelets, rings and brooches.

'Oh, how lovely!' cried Rosaline, as she saw them. 'I never did see anything quite so beautiful as your lovely stones, little man!'

'Well, I'm pleased to hear you say so,' said the elf, smiling. 'Now just choose anything you think you would like, and I shall be delighted to give it to you. One good turn deserves another.'

'You *are* kind,' said Rosaline, going red with delight. 'I haven't a ring, so do you think I might choose one?'

'Certainly,' said the little man. 'What colour?'

'Well, I have such a pretty green frock at home that I think I'd like a green one to match,' said Rosaline.

At once one of the elves ran over to her with a tray of bright-green rings. Rosaline picked one up and looked at it. It was set in silver and the green stone was very big and bright.

'May I have this one?' she asked.

'Yes,' said the elf. 'But I must just warn you of something, Rosaline, if you have that ring. Never tell an untruth while you are wearing it, for it can only belong to someone truthful.'

'Oh, I'll be very careful,' said Rosaline. She slipped the ring on her finger, and then followed the elf along the passage back to his little house again. She thanked him very much, said goodbye and ran home, delighted with her present. The ring shone brightly on her finger and was so beautiful that it caught everyone's eye.

Now the next day, when Rosaline went to school, all the girls and boys crowded round her to see the ring, for they soon noticed it on her finger.

'Where did you get it, where did you get it?' they cried.

Rosaline told them her story – but alas! – she

could not keep to the truth.

'The little man wanted a hundred sandwiches,' she said, 'and I cut them all in five minutes. Wasn't it clever of me? No wonder he wanted to give me a ring!'

Suddenly Rosaline gave a cry. The ring suddenly seemed to become much tighter and pressed so hard round her finger that it hurt her.

'Oh, Rosaline!' cried the children. 'Your ring has changed colour! Look! It has gone a fiery-red colour! How strange!'

So it had. It had lost its beautiful bright-green hue and was now a flaming, angry red. It was so tight that Rosaline couldn't get it off, and it hurt her very much.

Suddenly one of the children pointed his finger at her.

'I know, I know!' he cried. 'You've told a story and the ring's gone red for danger! Storyteller, storyteller!'

Rosaline went as red as the ring. She suddenly remembered the elf's warning, and she knew she had been foolish and wrong.

'I – I *did* tell a story,' she said humbly. 'I only made twenty sandwiches, not a hundred.'

At once the ring stopped squeezing her finger and became its proper size. It went dark for a moment, and then turned from red to its own bright green once again.

'It's green again, it's green again!' cried everyone. Rosaline looked at it in astonishment. What a peculiar ring!

I don't think I like it very much after all, she thought. *It will be dreadful if it keeps turning red like that.*

The ring remained green all that day, and then Rosaline forgot again. Her mother said it must be bedtime and sent Rosaline to see if it was half past six.

It was, but Rosaline didn't want to go to bed. So the naughty little girl told her mother that it was only ten minutes past the hour. No sooner had she told that story than the ring tightened on her finger again and made her cry out. It went fiery red, and Rosaline, frightened that her mother might see it, hastily told the truth.

'No, Mummy, I made a mistake,' she said. 'It *is* half past six, so I'd better go to bed.'

The ring loosened and became green once more. Rosaline kissed her mother goodnight and ran off.

That night in bed she had a long think. She wanted to wear the ring, for it was very beautiful, but she knew quite well that she could only do so safely if she stopped telling stories.

Well, it is *horrid to keep telling stories*, thought the little girl. *I'd much better stop, before I get too bad. And the ring will help me, for every time I feel it hurting me, I'll know I've not spoken truly, and I'll own up.*

She fell asleep comforted. But although it was easy to make up her mind to be good, it was dreadfully hard to get out of her bad habit. Rosaline was horrified to find how many times she told stories. Time after time she felt the ring tighten angrily on her finger, and saw it change to a fierce red, attracting everyone's attention to it.

'Storyteller, storyteller!' cried the children when they saw the ring change colour. 'Oh, you naughty little storyteller!'

Then Rosaline would go red too, and say she was sorry, and tell the truth properly. The ring would flash green again, while the children laughed. But little by little Rosaline learnt her lesson, and soon she became quite a truthful little girl.

She still has the ring, and if ever you meet her she will show it to you, and perhaps let you wear it for a few minutes. But if you are a storyteller, don't put it on – for the ring will turn a fiery red, and so will you!

He Bought a Secret

He Bought a Secret

TWO MAGICAL brownies were talking together as they went home. 'I tell you,' said Gobbo, 'I never saw such a mass of gold in my life – sheets of it!'

'I know,' said the other brownie. 'I've seen it too. And how it gleams in the sun! It's almost too bright to look at.'

They didn't know that the goblin Sharp-Eye was just behind them listening to every word! He was tiptoeing along, hearing all they said. How his eyes shone when he heard about this gold!

He pounced on the two brownies and caught them by their belts. He jerked them back, and they almost fell, wriggling in alarm.

'Now then!' said Gobbo. 'What's all this? Let go of my belt, Sharp-Eye.'

'And let me go too,' said Whiskers, the other brownie. 'What kind of behaviour is this?'

'Where's this gold you're talking about?' said Sharp-Eye. 'That's what I want to know. Tell me!'

'Certainly not,' said Gobbo at once. 'You're a greedy, miserly, selfish little goblin, who never gives a penny to anyone – why should we tell you where any gold is? You have far too much already!'

'Who does it belong to?' asked Sharp-Eye, still holding on to the brownies' belts.

'Nobody,' said Whiskers, wriggling.

Sharp-Eye laughed. 'I've never heard of gold that belonged to nobody,' he said. 'I shall go and get it then, and have it for myself. Where is it?'

'We're not going to tell you,' said Gobbo.

'It's a secret,' said Whiskers, giving a sly wink at Gobbo without Sharp-Eye seeing him.

'I'll buy the secret,' said Sharp-Eye.

'Pooh,' said Whiskers. 'You *say* you would – but when the time came to pay up, you wouldn't be anywhere to be seen! We know your promises! Didn't you promise to pay us five silver pieces to give to old Dame Jeanie when she was ill! But you didn't pay up. And didn't you promise to pay us a gold piece when Mr Old-Man's house caught on fire? But you didn't.'

'And who promised to pay two gold pieces when we wanted to buy a present for the princess Marygold's birthday?' said Gobbo. 'You did! But when we came to collect it you shut yourself in your house and pretended you weren't there. You're a mean creature, Sharp-Eye.'

'I tell you, I'll pay you for the secret,' said Sharp-Eye sulkily. 'I've got plenty of money with me today. I'll pay you now, this very minute.'

'Well, let go of our belts then,' said Gobbo. 'Your fingers are as hard and knobbly as your heart,

Sharp-Eye. My back feels bruised already. You're a nasty little fellow.'

Sharp-Eye let them go. 'Now tell me where this wonderful gold is,' he said 'Look – here's payment for you!' and he put his hand in his pocket and brought out a handful of money. Gobbo and Whiskers looked at it.

Then they looked at one another and winked and nodded their heads.

'Right,' said Gobbo. 'Now, let me think – little Tiptoe needs a holiday. Give us a gold piece for her. And Old Man Tiptap wants a new stick to help him get about. Give us five silver pieces for that.'

'Yes – and Mistress Nid-Nod lost her warm shawl the other day,' said Whiskers. 'Give us ten silver pieces to give her so that she can buy a new one. And let me see – I did hear that little Silver-Wings was sad because her kitten was stolen. Give us a silver piece for her.'

Sharp-Eye looked sulky, but he counted out

the money into Gobbo's hand. 'One gold piece for Tiptoe. Five silver pieces for Old Man Tiptap. Ten silver pieces for Mistress Nid-Nod, the horrid old thing. And one silver piece for Silver-Wings – though why she wants to get a nasty, scratchy kitten again, I can't think.'

'Thanks,' said Gobbo, and put the money into his pocket.

'Now where's this mass of gold?' said Sharp-Eye.

'Go through the wood – turn down the lane – go to the end – climb over the stile there – and you will see the gold,' said Whiskers with a grin. 'There'll be too much for you to take, Sharp-Eye – you'll have to be content with a handful.'

Sharp-Eye thought this sounded wonderful. He darted off at once. He went through the wood and down the lane to the end. He climbed over the stile and looked for the gold.

He was in a buttercup field. All round him, and as far as he could see, a mass of gold buttercups nodded and shone. They were dazzling in the sunshine, and so beautiful that the children always went that way home from school just so that they could see them.

But Sharp-Eye didn't think they were beautiful. He was after gold, and buttercups were just a nuisance. Perhaps the gold was hidden at the foot of their green stems? He went into the field and began to kick about the buttercups, trying to find the gold he was looking for.

Soon he had kicked a hundred shining buttercups down, but he had found no gold. Then he heard a shout.

'Hey, you! What do you think you're doing, spoiling those buttercups?'

'I've come to find the gold in this field,' yelled back Sharp-Eye angrily. 'But I can't see any. Someone must have taken it – and I paid for the secret too.'

There was a loud laugh. Sharp-Eye turned to see who had been shouting and laughing. He saw Dame Sturdy standing at the stile. He didn't like her and he made a face.

'Have *you* taken the gold?' he yelled.

'No, it's there, all round you!' called back Dame Sturdy. 'Buttercup gold, the loveliest gold in the world! Sheets and sheets of it, dazzling and bright. Better than the gold *you're* so fond of, you mean little goblin!'

And then Sharp-Eye knew that Gobbo and Whiskers had tricked him! This was the gold they had been talking about, this was the gold they had meant – buttercup gold, that belonged to nobody – and yet belonged to everybody!

He was so angry that he stamped on the buttercups round him. Quickly Dame Sturdy was over the stile and had hold of him. She dragged him out of the field.

'No one treats buttercups like that when *I'm* about,' she said. 'Now you're going to get told off, Sharp-Eye, so get ready to say sorry! Are you ready? Well, then – one, two, three, go!'

You should have heard the goblin wail! He couldn't get away until Dame Sturdy had punished him, and then he ran off, crying.

'I gave Gobbo and Whiskers all that money for the secret – and all I got was silly buttercups and a telling-off! I *am* an unlucky fellow, to be sure!'

So he was. But mean people are always unlucky – and a very good thing too!

Thirty-Three Candles

Thirty-Three Candles

'I DON'T want Yah to come to my birthday party,' said Twinks. 'I don't like him.'

'Oh, but we must ask him!' said Twinks's mother. 'He'll be so offended if we don't. He might do all sorts of horrible things to us.'

'He's a nasty, horrid, unkind goblin,' wailed Twinks. 'He'll spoil my party!'

'Well, he'll blow our house down, or make our hens disappear or something like that if we leave him out of the party,' said Mrs Twinks. 'Anyway, he'll be sure to do lots of tricks at the party – he's very good at those, just as good as a conjuror.'

'I don't like him or his tricks, and I won't like my party,' said poor Twinks gloomily.

All the same, Mrs Twinks knew she had to ask Yah. He was a very powerful little goblin, and goodness knows what he would do if he wasn't asked.

The day of the party came. Mrs Twinks had made all kinds of sandwiches, cakes, biscuits and jellies. She had made a birthday cake too, with thirty-three candles on it. Although Twinks was very small, elves are not grown up until they are more than a hundred years old, so thirty-three was really quite young for an elf.

Yah came with the other guests, dressed in a magnificent sparkling suit.

'It is made of flames, sewn with snippings of moonlight and then damped down a bit with mist,' he said. 'Nice, isn't it?'

He looked round at the tea table. 'Ah – not a bad spread, Mrs Twinks. Would you like to see me eat a whole plateful of sausage rolls at one gulp?'

Mrs Twinks didn't want to see that at all, and neither did anyone else. Those lovely sausage rolls! Everyone wanted one of those! Yah beckoned with his fingers and opened his mouth wide – and one by one the sausage rolls flew through the air and straight into his mouth! 'What a waste!' whispered poor Twinks to his mother.

'Very nice,' said Yah, and sat down at the table. He caught sight of the balloons hanging all around the room. 'Ah – have you seen my new trick of sending sharp looks at balloons – so sharp that they burst? Ha, ha, ha!'

'You couldn't do that!' said Twinks. 'Sharp looks wouldn't burst balloons!'

But they did! Every time Yah looked sharply at a balloon it went pop! Soon there were no balloons left. Twinks was almost in tears. His mother frowned at him. She hoped he wasn't going to be rude to Yah. Oh, dear – Yah was such a nuisance!

'Ah – jellies!' said Yah. 'Have you ever seen jellies

playing leap-frog?'

'No – and I don't want to,' said Twinks crossly. 'Leave them alone!'

But, no – Yah did a bit of magic, the jellies jumped over one another, and before long there was one big mix-up of jellies in a dish, all wobbling and shivering in fright.

'They'll taste horrid,' said Twinks. 'Mother, stop him. He's being silly. He's not being clever! Mother, please light the candles on my cake. It's time they were lit.'

'You think I'm silly, not clever, do you?' said Yah, glaring at him. 'Well then, I'll turn myself into a little flame and light every single one of your thirty-three candles!'

And before anyone could say 'Please don't!' Yah had disappeared, and a tiny yellow flame appeared in the air over the big iced birthday cake. Everyone watched in amazement. Yes – that was really clever of Yah!

All round the cake went the little magic flame, lighting one candle after another.

A tiny voice called out, 'Aren't I clever? I'm Yah the goblin, the cleverest in the world! I'm a burning flame. One candle, two, three – twenty-one – twenty-nine – thirty-two – now watch when I get to the last one. I'll sit on it myself, a little goblin-flame!'

And now all the candles were alight, and burning merrily. Yah's flame sat on the last candle, bigger and brighter than the others.

'Mother,' said Twinks suddenly. 'Birthday candles always have to be blown out, don't they? And if I wish when I blow them out, my wish comes true, doesn't it?'

'Only if you blow them all out at once,' said his mother. 'I don't think anyone could blow out thirty-three candles in one blow. Don't try! Yah would be angry.'

'Yes, very angry!' called the little high-burning voice from Yah's own flame. 'Let the candles burn down and I will blow them out!'

'But it's my cake!' shouted Twinks, and he took an enormous breath. Then he blew the breath out of his mouth with a great big blow! *Whoooooooooosh!*

They started going out – half went out – some more went out – and then there was only one left. Twinks only had a little of his one big blow left – but it was enough. The last candle went out – the one that Yah had sat himself on as a little flame. The candles sent tiny spires of smoke up – they were all out! Nobody said a word.

Then Mrs Twinks spoke. 'Yah! Where are you? I'm so sorry Twinks blew like that. Please don't punish him!'

There was no answer. Twinks giggled. 'Mother,' he said, 'don't you know what's happened? I've blown Yah out too, like all the candle flames! I don't know where flames go to – but wherever it is, Yah is with them. He isn't here any more – and he'll never come back. When I blew the candles out I wished that he would vanish for ever!'

'Twinks has got rid of him!' shouted his friends, and danced round the room. 'Horrid old Yah! He's gone!'

Well – Yah certainly didn't come back. It was most extraordinary. Laughing happily, the guests began to eat the birthday tea again, and how they enjoyed it without Yah there to spoil things for them. Nobody lit the candles again though. They thought that Yah might come back again if they did!

But he never did come back, and Twinks was made a great fuss of after that.

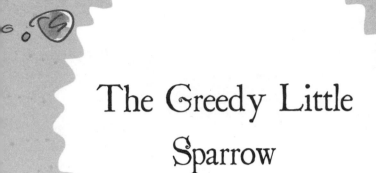

The Greedy Little
Sparrow

The Greedy Little Sparrow

FEATHERS WAS a greedy little brown sparrow who was always first on the bird table and last to go. How he loved the crusts, bacon rinds and scraps that Hannah and Frank put out every morning!

He wished he could keep all the other birds away from the table so that he might have even more to eat. But how could he do that?

'I know!' he said at last. 'I'll say that the black cat is about. Then the others will be careful and I shall be able to eat all I want to.'

So the next morning, when Hannah and Frank put food on their bird table, Feathers began to chirrup loudly to the others.

'Chirrup! Chirrup! Be careful! Be careful! Chirrup! The cat's about! Chirrup! She's hiding under a bush; I saw her! Chirrup! She is waiting for us to go on the bird table and then she will pounce! Chirrup!'

All the birds heard this warning cry and stayed quietly in the bushes and on the gutter. Everyone was afraid of the cat. No one wanted to be caught by Cosy, whose sharp claws could strike down even a big bird like Glossy the blackbird.

'I'll fly down to the bird table and see if Cosy is anywhere about still!' Feathers chirruped shortly.

'Keep where you are, everybody! I'll fly down!' He flew down – and in a second was pecking hard at the breadcrumbs there. 'Chirrup!' he called to the others. 'Be careful! I think I can see the cat under the lilac bush! I'll tell you when she goes!'

Feathers had another good peck at the food, pretending to keep a watch for the cat every now and again. The other birds watched him hungrily – but no one ventured to fly down. They were dreadfully afraid of Cosy the cat.

Then the starling, who had been sitting on the chimney top warming his toes, suddenly gave a splutter. 'Why! There's Cosy in the next-door garden! She can't be hiding under the lilac bush!'

Sure enough, when the birds looked, there was Cosy lying peacefully in the next garden, asleep in the sun. One by one the birds flew down to the table and were soon enjoying a good meal. But Feathers had taken all the best titbits, you may be sure.

The next day Feathers went on with his trick. As soon as Hannah and Frank had filled the bird table with scraps, and the birds had flown down to them, Feathers, who was sitting on the gutter, gave a loud chirrup.

'Chirrup! Chirrup! Fly away quickly! I can see a tabby cat round by that tub! He's watching you all! He's going to pounce! Chirrup!'

With a flutter of wings and squawks of fright all

the sparrows, chaffinches, starlings and thrushes flew off the bird table. Some went to the bushes, some flew to the roof and others were so frightened that they flew to the fields. Feathers was pleased. He flew down to the bird table at once and called to the others.

'I'll keep my eye on that tabby cat! I can see him from here! I'll tell you when he's gone! Oh, you bad cat, I can see you, yes, I can see you! Chirrup, chirrup!'

'Isn't Feathers brave?' said a little chaffinch with a bright-pink chest.

'He's wonderful the way he sees any hiding cat,' said a cock-sparrow.

'And it's very plucky of him to wait on the table and tell us when the cat is gone,' said a gleaming starling. 'That cat might easily pounce on him.'

Feathers heard what everyone was saying and he chirruped in delight to himself. He was doing something very mean – and here were the others praising him and thinking him such a fine, brave fellow.

I'm clever, I am, thought Feathers. *They're all foolish.*

I'm the only clever one. See how easily I am tricking them! I keep them all away from the food till I've taken the best.

He pecked away busily, pretending to keep an eye on the cat all the time. Then, when he had eaten all the best scraps, he chirruped to the others, 'You can come down to the table safely now, for the cat has gone. I saw him slink away. He's afraid of me!'

The birds flew down and fed. They were very polite to Feathers, for they all thought he was a charming and helpful fellow.

The next day Feathers spied some cake crumbs in the next-door-but-one garden. He loved these, for they were sweet. The children had eaten their tea in the garden and had left a great many cake crumbs about. Feathers was pleased.

'Nobody else seems to have seen them,' said Feathers to himself. 'That's lucky. I shan't share them with anyone. I'll just fly down and get them.'

As he was about to fly down, a small hen-sparrow chirruped to him from the roof, 'Feathers! Feathers!

Be careful! There is a big Persian cat in the garden! Don't go down for those cake crumbs!'

'Oho!' said Feathers to himself, with a quick look round. 'So there is another sparrow who is playing my trick and pretending there are cats about so that she can get the crumbs herself! No, no, little hen-sparrow – you can't trick me like that. I'm too clever.'

He flew down to the crumbs and began to peck them up. The little hen-sparrow on the roof hopped up and down in the greatest excitement and fear.

'Feathers! The cat is there! Come back, come back! Eat the crumbs later when the cat is gone!'

Feathers took no notice. He went on pecking up the crumbs, which were really delicious. That little hen-sparrow could be as clever as she liked – he wasn't going to take any notice.

But the hen-sparrow was not being clever – she was being kind. The cat really was there! And suddenly poor Feathers knew it, for there came a soft rustle –

and the Persian cat pounced on the greedy little sparrow.

It would have been the end of Feathers if the little hen-sparrow on the roof hadn't made such a noise. Lucy, the little girl that the cat belonged to, heard the noise and came running out. Feathers flew off with almost no feathers in his tail.

Poor Feathers! It was a punishment for greediness and untruthfulness. He thought he was so clever – but he wasn't even clever enough to know that it is foolish to be greedy and to tell untruths.

If you see a little sparrow with a rather short tail, have a look at him. It might be Feathers.

The Magic Clock

The Magic Clock

ONCE WHEN Jinky went by Mother Goody's, he saw her nice round-faced clock.

Now Jinky had no clock, and he had always wanted one like Mother Goody's. He peeped in at the kitchen door. There was no one inside. Then the naughty little fellow ran to the mantelpiece, took down the clock, hid it under his coat and ran home.

'Mother Goody has two clocks, so she can spare me this one,' said Jinky to himself. 'But I'd better not put it on my mantelpiece in case anyone comes in and sees it. I will hide it.'

So he put it in his larder. No sooner had he

done that than Dame Fanny came in for a chat. Jinky gave her a chair and they sat talking away for a long time – but as they talked, a curious noise was gradually heard.

It was the noise of ticking – but, dear me, *such* loud ticking! 'TICK-TOCK! TICK-TOCK! TICK-TOCK!'

'What's that noise?' said Dame Fanny, looking round in surprise.

'What noise?' said Jinky, going red and wondering why ever the clock ticked so loudly.

'That loud sort of tick-tock noise,' said Dame Fanny. 'I can't see a clock anywhere. It seems to come from your larder too – how strange, Jinky! What can it be?'

'Oh, just the cat in there, I expect,' said Jinky, still very red. 'Don't you think you ought to be going now, Dame Fanny? I believe I heard the bus coming!'

Dame Fanny jumped up in a hurry, forgetting all about the noise. She said goodbye and ran down the path. Jinky was glad to see her go. He went to the larder, opened the door and glared at the clock, which was now ticking softly again.

'You horrible thing!' said Jinky. 'I suppose you thought you'd let Dame Fanny know you were here! Well, to punish you I'll just take you upstairs to my bedroom and put you into the dark wardrobe. Then nobody can hear you ticking.'

So he took the clock upstairs and put it into his wardrobe. He shut the door loudly. When he got downstairs he found his friend Peter Penny there.

'Hallo!' said Peter. 'Can I have a drink of lemonade, Jinky? I'm so thirsty.'

Jinky poured out a drink – and just as he was doing it, there came the sound of a bell ringing loudly. 'R-r-r-r-r-ring, r-r-r-r-r-ring, r-r-r-r-r-ring!'

'Good gracious, what's that?' said Peter, jumping. He spilt the lemonade in fright.

'Must be someone at the front door,' said Jinky. But there wasn't anybody there. The bell rang again, even more loudly. 'Rr-r-r-ring! R-r-r-r-r-ring!'

'Perhaps it's someone at the *back* door,' said Peter Penny. But there was nobody there either.

Still the bell went on ringing and ringing. 'Sounds like an alarm clock going off,' said Peter, puzzled. 'But you haven't got a clock, have you, Jinky?'

Jinky went red and didn't answer. Of course, the noise was made by that tiresome clock! Still it went on ringing.

'I don't think I like it, Jinky,' said Peter, getting up. 'It's very strange – a bell ringing like that and nobody at the door. Goodbye!'

Jinky tore upstairs to the clock and took it out of the wardrobe. It stopped ringing and looked up at him with a cheeky round face. It waved its hands at him and then clapped them together.

'Tick-tock, I gave you a shock!' ticked the clock, and clapped its hands again.

'*You're* going to get a shock now,' said naughty Jinky, and he took the clock down to the dustbin. He put it inside and clapped the lid on it. 'There!

Now the dustman can take you when he comes!'

But the clock didn't mind. It ticked loudly in the dustbin, it ran its bell as loudly as an ice-cream man's, and it jumped up and down against the tin lid of the dustbin, making a tremendous noise.

Mother Goody heard the noise as she passed by, and she called in at Jinky's window. 'Jinky! There's such a funny noise in your dustbin. What have you got there?'

Jinky got such a shock when he heard Mother Goody's voice that he didn't know what to say. At last he stammered out, 'Oh, it's only the c-c-c-cat, I expect, Mother G-Goody.'

'The *cat*! In the *dust*bin! With the *lid* on!' cried Mother Goody in astonishment. 'I never heard of such a thing! You just come and get that cat out, Jinky!'

She took Jinky by the collar and dragged him to the dustbin. She took off the lid – and there was her own round-faced clock staring up at her, ticking and ringing and clapping its hands for joy!

'So *that* was what it was!' said Mother Goody. 'I met Dame Fanny and Peter Penny this morning, and they both told me what strange noises they heard in your house. I suppose you stole my clock, and when it wouldn't be quiet, you put the poor thing into the dustbin.'

'Please forgive me,' wept Jinky, very much afraid.

'Oh, I'll forgive you all right,' said Mother Goody. 'But I think you're a very rubbishy sort of person, Jinky – and rubbish goes into the dustbin, doesn't it? Well – in you go! Goodbye!'

And Mother Goody put Jinky into the dustbin, clapped the big lid over him and, taking her clock under her arm, went off home, smiling all over her face.

'He won't steal things again in a hurry!' said Mother Goody. 'He'll have to stay there till the dustman comes this afternoon!'

'Tock-tick, tock-tick! What a very pretty trick,' said the clock to Mother Goody. And you should have heard them both laugh!

The Little Tease

The Little Tease

'NOW YOU look after Bobby for a little while, Betty,' said Mummy, going out of the playroom door. 'Don't tease him, he's so little – play with him nicely.'

Betty set out the bricks and began to build a castle with them. Bobby helped. Then they wound up the clockwork car and set it going, and it raced round and round the room, bumping at last into a table leg and stopping very suddenly.

Betty soon got tired of playing with Bobby, and took a book to read. Bobby tried to shut the book. 'Play with me,' he said. 'Mummy said so.'

'Don't,' said Betty and snatched the book away.

Bobby went to the window and looked out into the garden.

'The sun's shining,' he said. 'We can go out now. Mummy said so. I want to go out.'

'Do be quiet,' said Betty.

'I'll call Mummy,' said Bobby. 'I'll tell her I want to go out.'

Betty wanted to read. She didn't want to go out. That meant putting on Bobby's coat and hat and outdoor shoes.

'We can't go out,' she said. 'There are dragons in the garden.'

'There aren't,' said Bobby, looking scared.

'Yes, there are. And there are lions too,' said Betty. 'And both dragons and lions roar. They might jump at you, Bobby. We won't go into the garden yet.'

'There aren't any lions and dragons in the garden,' said Bobby, frowning. 'Mummy didn't say so. You're a fibber, Betty.'

'How *dare* you call me a fibber!' said Betty, glaring

at Bobby. 'You bad boy! I tell you, it's perfectly true, there *are* lions and dragons in the garden!'

'I don't like hearing about them,' said Bobby. 'I'm going down to Mummy.'

'You just stay here,' said Betty. 'Else I'll tell the lions about you.' The door suddenly opened, and Uncle Don came into the room. He looked very stern. 'Betty,' he said, 'I couldn't help hearing all this about lions and dragons, and I'm ashamed to think you could tease Bobby like that. What dreadful fibs!'

Betty went red. 'They're not fibs,' she said. 'I really meant the snap*dragons* and the dande*lions*, Uncle Don. They're only flowers.'

'I see!' said Uncle Don. 'But you didn't mean *Bobby* to think that your lions and dragons were only flowers! I'm really ashamed of you!'

'I don't care!' said Betty rudely. 'I only meant *flowers*, I tell you!'

Uncle Don took Bobby downstairs with him. Betty began to feel scared. Uncle Don would tell

Mummy – and Mummy might be very, very cross! Perhaps cross enough to scold her, and Betty didn't like that.

She decided to slip downstairs and out of the side door into the garden. She would hide in the shed till Uncle Don had gone. So very soon she was sitting in the shed with her book.

And it was while she was sitting there that she suddenly heard the strange noise. It sounded like something growling in the bushes outside the shed. Betty put down her book and listened. Was it a dog? The next-door dog, perhaps? She hoped not because she had teased it several times and it didn't like her!

Betty got up and shut the shed door. She felt safer then. She took up her book, but she soon put it down again when she heard another noise.

This time it was a kind of roaring! Whatever could it be? She peeped out of the shed window but she couldn't see anything. Then she heard the growling again and felt scared.

Oh, dear – if Bobby were here he would say it was the lions and dragons I frightened him about, thought Betty. *It sounds like them! I wish I'd never said such a thing to him!*

The growling came again, even nearer to the shed. Betty looked out of the window, trembling. She couldn't see anything – except Bobby, standing on the back-door steps some way away.

She shouted to him. 'Bobby, Bobby! There's some fierce animal in the bushes here and I'm afraid to come out of the shed! Fetch Mummy, quickly!'

But Bobby didn't. He looked scared first of all – and then he suddenly ran down the garden at top speed. 'I'll save you, I'll save you!' he cried. 'It's the lions and the dragons you told me about. I'll kill them, and save you, Betty, don't be afraid!'

And the five-year-old Bobby pulled aside the bush near the shed to find a dragon or a lion! He meant to save his sister if he could.

There wasn't an animal there – there was only Uncle Don! Yes, it was he who had growled and roared, to teach Betty what it was like to be frightened! He smiled at Bobby and hugged him. 'Betty!' he called, 'come out! You're safe now. Bobby has found the lions and the dragons and you're quite safe.'

Betty came out in surprise. 'Oh, Uncle Don – was it *you* who frightened me so? You *are* unkind!'

'There's no difference between us, Betty,' said Uncle Don. 'You're a *little* tease – I'm a *big* one. But what do you think of Bobby, coming to fight dragons and lions so that he could save you – after you'd teased and frightened him so? Not many little brothers would have been brave enough to do that.'

Betty suddenly felt ashamed of herself. She looked at Bobby's round, solemn face. 'Thank you, Bobby,' she said. 'I'm sorry I teased you, I really am. I didn't deserve to be saved by you – I think you're very, very brave.'

'Well said, Betty!' said Uncle Don, sounding very pleased. 'You're not such a horrid child as I thought you were, after all. Now let's leave the lions and the dragons to blossom peacefully in the sun and go indoors and have our dinner!'

'Woo-how-ow-ow!' roared Bobby, and made them both jump. 'I'm just saying goodbye to them in their language,' he told the astonished Betty. 'I don't mind those lions now. We'll come and play with them this afternoon. Woo-how-ow-ow!'

But isn't it funny – Betty will NOT play lions and dragons however much Bobby begs her to. Do you think she has frightened herself with her own story? I wouldn't be surprised.

It Was the Wind!

TRICKY AND Dob lived next door to one another. Dob was a hard-working little fellow, always busy about something. Tricky was a scamp, and he teased the life out of poor old Dob.

He undid the clothes from Dob's washing line so that they dropped into the mud. He crept through a hole in his fence and took the eggs that Feathers, Dob's white hen, laid for him. He borrowed this and he borrowed that – but he always forgot to return anything.

Dob put up with Tricky and his ways very patiently, but he did wish Tricky didn't live next to him! He didn't like Tricky at all, but he didn't tell tales or complain about him, so nobody ever punished Tricky or scolded him.

Still, things can't go on like that for ever, and one day a very funny thing happened. It was an autumn day, and the leaves had blown down from the trees, spreading all over Dob's garden. They were making Tricky's garden untidy too, of course, but he didn't mind a bit. Dob did mind. He was a good little gardener and he loved his garden to be tidy and neat.

So he took his broom and began to sweep his leaves into a big heap. He swept them up by the fence between his garden and Tricky's. There! Now his garden was tidy again. Dob went to fetch his barrow to put the leaves into it to take down to the rubbish heap.

Tricky had been watching Dob sweeping up his leaves. He grinned. Dob had put the pile of leaves just by the hole in the fence! Tricky slipped out as soon as Dob had gone to fetch his barrow, and went to his fence.

He wriggled through the hole into the middle of the pile of leaves. Then he scattered all the leaves over the grass and crept back unseen through the hole.

Dob will be surprised! he thought. And Dob was. He was annoyed as well. What had happened? A minute ago the leaves had been in a neat pile – now they were all over the place again!

He saw Tricky looking over the fence. 'Good day, Dob,' said Tricky politely. 'It's a pity the wind blew your leaves away just as you got them into a pile, wasn't it?'

'The wind?' said Dob, puzzled. 'But there isn't any wind.'

'Well, it must have been a sudden mischievous breeze then,' said Tricky, grinning. 'You know – a little young wind that doesn't know any better.'

'Hmm!' said Dob, and he swept up all his leaves into a pile again. It was lunchtime then, so he left them and went indoors. But he didn't get his lunch at once. He just watched behind his curtain to see if that tiresome Tricky came into his garden to kick away his pile of leaves.

Well, he didn't see Tricky, of course, because that mischievous fellow had wriggled through the hole in the fence which was well hidden by the pile of leaves. He was now in the very middle of the pile – and to Dob's enormous surprise the leaves suddenly shot up into the air and flew all over the grass.

'What a very peculiar thing!' said Dob, astonished. 'I've never seen leaves behave like that before. Can it be that Tricky is right, and that a little breeze is playing about with them?'

He thought about it while he ate his lunch. It couldn't be Tricky, because Dob hadn't seen him climb over the fence and go to the pile. One minute the pile had been there, neat and tidy – and the next it had been scattered all over the place.

I'll sweep up the leaves once more, thought Dob. *And I'll put them into my barrow before that wind gets them again.*

But of course Tricky got into the next pile too, through the hole in the fence and was now back in his own garden, grinning away at Dob.

'My word – are you still sweeping up leaves? There's no end to it, Dob.'

'I think you must have been right when you said that the wind is playing tricks with me,' said Dob. 'But the thing is, what am I to do about it?'

'Catch the bad fellow and make him prisoner!' said Tricky.

'But how can you catch the wind?' asked Dob.

'Well, haven't you seen how the wind loves to billow out a sail, or blow out a sack or a balloon?' said Tricky. 'Just get a sack, Dob, put the wind in it when he next comes along, tie up the neck and send him off by carrier to the weatherman to deal with. He'll give him a punishment, you may be sure!'

'Well – if I could catch the wind that way I would certainly do all you say,' said Dob. 'But I'm afraid it isn't possible.'

All the same, he went and got a sack and put it ready nearby in case the wind did come along again. Tricky watched him sweep up his leaves once more, and he simply couldn't resist creeping through the hole to play the same trick on poor old Dob again!

But this time Dob was on the watch for the wind, and as soon as he saw the leaves just beginning to stir, he clapped the sack over the pile. He felt something wriggling in the leaves and gave a shout. 'I've got him! I've caught the wind! He's filling up my sack! Aha, you scamp of a wind, I've got you!'

Tricky wriggled and shouted in the sack, but Dob shook him well down to the bottom of it, together with dozens of leaves, and tied up the neck firmly with rope.

'It's no good wriggling and shouting like that!' he said sternly. 'You're caught. It's a good thing Tricky told me how to catch you! Now, off to the weatherman you're going, and goodness knows what he'll do with you!'

He wrote a big label:

TO BE DELIVERED TO THE WEATHERMAN BY
THE CARRIER – ONE SMALL, MISCHIEVOUS
BREEZE. SUGGEST IT SHOULD BE WELL
PUNISHED BEFORE IT IS ALLOWED TO
BLOW AGAIN.

And when the carrier came by with his cart, Dob handed the whimpering Tricky to him, tightly tied up in the sack. The carrier read the label and grinned.

'I'll deliver him, all right,' he said. 'The weatherman isn't in a very good temper lately – I'm afraid he will punish this little breeze hard.'

Dob went to look over the fence to find Tricky and tell him that his good idea had been carried out – but Tricky was nowhere to be seen, of course! And he was nowhere to be seen for three whole days! Dob was very puzzled.

He came back the evening of the third day. He

looked very solemn indeed. The weatherman had punished him well and truly, and had set him to do all kinds of blowing jobs, which made Tricky very much out of breath.

'Hallo, Tricky! Wherever have you been?' cried Dob.

Tricky wouldn't tell him. He wouldn't tell anyone. But everyone agreed that his three days away had done him good – he wasn't nearly so mischievous, and ever since that day he has never played a single trick on old Dob.

'I can't imagine why!' said Dob. How he would laugh if he knew!

Amelia Jane and the Soap

Amelia Jane and the Soap

AMELIA JANE was feeling very bored. She had behaved herself for a whole week!

'But only because she hasn't been able to think of anything naughty to do,' said Tom to Teddy. 'As soon as she thinks of something she'll cheer up and be as bad as ever.'

Well, it wasn't long before Amelia Jane did cheer up. She had thought of something.

You see, it was like this – she had gone out for a nice walk, sitting in her doll's pram, and she had been taken into the town. Now, racing up and down the pavement were two boys on roller skates. What a pace they went!

Amelia Jane leant out of the pram to watch them. She thought it was a lovely game. She tried to see what the boys had on their feet, but they went so fast that Amelia Jane really didn't see what the skates were like.

How do *they slip along so fast?* she thought. *I would like to skate like that. How I wish I could! I'd go round and round the nursery, and down the passage and back. My, wouldn't the toys stare!*

Now, when Amelia Jane had an idea she just had to carry it out. So when she got back to the nursery she sat at the back of the toy cupboard and thought hard.

I want to skate, she said to herself. *I want to put something on my feet and slip along like those boys. I want to go fast! But what can I put on my feet?*

'What are you thinking so hard about?' asked the clockwork clown, poking his head in at the door.

'Never you mind,' said Amelia Jane.

'Tell me and maybe I can help,' said the clown.

'Well, I'm trying to think of something nice and slippery,' said Amelia Jane.

'What about jelly?' said the clown.

'Don't be silly,' said Amelia.

'Well, soap,' said the clown. 'Nice wet soap! Why, the other day I got hold of some wet soap and squeezed it – and it shot out of my hand like lightning and hit Tom on the ear!'

Amelia Jane laughed. Then she stopped and thought quickly. Soap! Yes – that was really a *good* idea! If she got two nice pieces of soap, made them wet and slippery and tied them under her feet, she would be able to slip along just like those boys on skates! Good!

'I'll try it!' said Amelia Jane. So she ran out of the toy cupboard and went to the nursery basin. She climbed up and looked to see if there was any soap there. There was – and what luck! – it had broken into two nice pieces.

'Oooh!' said Amelia in delight. 'Just what I want!'

She turned on the tap and wetted the soap till it was

so slippery she could hardly hold it. Then she climbed down with it. The toys looked at her in amazement.

'What are you going to do?' said Teddy. 'Are you going to give yourself a good wash for once?'

'Don't be rude,' said Amelia. 'You'll see in a minute what I'm going to do.'

She took off a hair ribbon and tore it in two. Naughty Amelia! Then she tied one piece of soap under her right foot and the other piece under her left foot. The toys stared at her as if they thought she was mad.

'Amelia, that's a funny way of washing your feet,' said Tom at last.

'I'm not washing my feet. I'm going to *skate*!' said Amelia proudly. 'Turn back the carpet, somebody. I must skate on the polished floor.'

The toys began to giggle. Really, what *would* Amelia Jane do next! Teddy and Tom turned back the carpet. Unfortunately they rolled the clockwork mouse up in it and had to unroll it again to get him out.

'Oh, do be quick!' said Amelia impatiently. 'I am simply longing to begin!'

At last the carpet was rolled right back. Amelia Jane began. She put first one foot out – slid along a little way on the soap – then put the other foot forward and slid too – and before the toys knew what she was about, there she was, skating round the nursery on her soap-skates!

How the toys laughed! Really, it was too funny to see Amelia sliding along so fast on pieces of soap!

Amelia Jane tried to stop – but she toppled and fell over, bang! The toys roared. It was funny to watch Amelia sitting down, plop, glaring at them angrily.

'How dare you laugh at me!' cried Amelia Jane. 'I shall go and learn how to skate in the passage. There is a nice polished floor there – I shall slide beautifully!'

'No, stay here,' said the clown in alarm. 'You know quite well that somebody may go along that passage and see you, Amelia Jane.'

'Pooh, everyone's in bed,' said Amelia, and this was true, for it was past midnight. 'Anyway, you won't be able to laugh at me there, if I fall down – for none of you dares to come into the passage.'

It was dark in the passage, for only a small light burnt there. Amelia slid out on her soap-skates and began to slide merrily up and down, up and down! The kitchen cat, hearing the noise, came creeping up the stairs, wondering if there was an extra-large-size mouse anywhere about.

He *was* astonished when he saw Amelia. He ran along the passage to see what she had on her feet. Amelia didn't hear him or see him, and she suddenly bumped right into him. Crash! She fell over and banged her head against the bedroom door.

'Sh! Amelia Jane! Sh!' whispered Tom, putting his head out of the nursery door. But Amelia Jane wouldn't hush. She got up angrily and shooed the cat away. But the cat spat and hissed, which scared her a bit.

If Amelia Jane had been sensible she would have run back to the nursery at once, but she was so keen on skating that she once more began to slide up and down, up and down, all along the passage. She didn't hear Nanny's bed creaking. She didn't hear Nanny creeping to the door. She didn't even see Nanny poking her head round the door – no, she went slipping and sliding up and down on the soap, having a perfectly lovely time!

Nanny couldn't make out who or what it was, for the passage was so dark. But she could quite well see something going up and down the passage, skating quickly. She moved to the light switch to put a brighter light on.

Amelia Jane saw her then. Quick as lightning the doll slipped through the nursery door, fell over on the carpet, tore off the bits of soap and ran to the toy cupboard. She climbed in on top of the bear and the clown, who were very angry at being walked on.

But nobody dared to say a word! Suppose Nanny

had seen what was happening? But when Nanny turned on the big light, all she saw was the kitchen cat sitting calmly by the wall.

'Good gracious,' she said, 'so it was *you* I saw, Puss, skating up and down the passage! What do you mean by doing that in the middle of the night, I should like to know! My goodness, what is the world coming to, when cats take to sliding up and down passages and waking everybody up! Shoo! Shoo!'

She shooed the cat down the stairs, and he disappeared quickly, tail in the air, boiling with rage to think that Amelia Jane had slipped off and left him to take the blame.

And in the morning when Nanny saw the messy bits of soap lying on the carpet, she was crosser than ever.

'Just look at that!' she said to Jane, the cleaner. 'It must be that cat. Slipped and slid down the passage all night long like a mad thing – and then went and tried to eat the soap out of the basin!'

Poor Puss got a scolding! Amelia Jane laughed at him – but she didn't laugh quite so much when the cat came downstairs and tore her new dress with his sharp claws.

'You'd better not skate any more with the soap, Amelia Jane,' said Tom. 'It's funny to watch you – but if you get other people into trouble it's not fair!'

So that was the end of Amelia Jane skating on the soap. I would have loved to see her, wouldn't you?

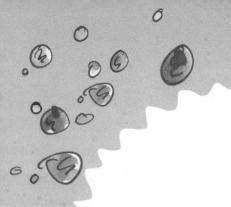

Here Comes the Wizard!

Here Comes the Wizard!

ONCE THERE was a wizard who used to live in a cave on High-Up Hill. But that was a very long time ago, so long that not one of the magical brownies who went up and down the hill could remember him.

But whenever they came back from the market one or other always said the same thing: 'It's a good thing the Wizard of Woolamalooloo is gone! We've so many goods with us that he would have a good haul if he popped out of his cave and stopped us!'

Then they would all laugh, because nobody lived in the cave now, certainly not a wizard.

The path to the market lay up the hill and down,

and passed near the old cave. The brownies loved going to market each Friday and coming back with all the things they had bought for their wives and children.

One day a new brownie came to live in Whispering Wood with the others. His name was Smarty, and he certainly was smart. He got better bargains at the market than anyone else.

When he heard the story of the old wizard who once lived in the cave, he thought about it. The next time the brownies walked down the hill near the cave, bringing home their goods from the market, Smarty listened to hear the usual remark. It came!

'It's a good thing the Wizard of Woolamalooloo is gone. We've so many goods that he would have a good haul if he popped out of his cave and stopped us.'

Then Smarty spoke in a very solemn voice. 'The Wizard of Woolamalooloo has come to live not far from here. I knew him before I came – a most unpleasant fellow. And he told me that one day he might come back here, hide in his cave and pop out at us coming back from market.'

Everyone looked most alarmed. 'I don't believe it,' said Stouty, a burly, good-natured little brownie.

'Ho!' said Smarty. 'You don't? Well, all I can say is this – that if ever any one of us yells out that he can see the old wizard waiting for us, we'd better drop our goods and run down the hill for all we're worth.'

'Stuff and nonsense!' said Stouty.

'I don't know,' said little Peeko. 'If the old wizard *is* about, and comes here, I think Smarty's idea is a good one. If we try to run away carrying our heavy goods, we'd soon be caught. Far better to drop our things and go!'

'Well spoken,' said Smarty. 'Well, I've warned you. We'll all keep a watch the very next time, in case the wizard is around! I've a feeling he may be!'

Stouty looked at Smarty and thought a lot. That wizard wouldn't come! Smarty was making it all up for some reason or other. What was the reason? Stouty rather thought he knew!

Now, on the next market day, all the brownies, except Stouty, went to market as usual, and back again. Smarty went too, of course. They came back up the hill, and then went down the other side, keeping a sharp lookout for the wizard.

And suddenly Smarty's voice rang out loudly. 'There he is! Behind those trees! I can see him lying in wait for us. Drop your things and run, brownies, run, Run, RUN!'

The brownies shrieked and yelled. They dropped all the goods they had bought and ran down the hill at top speed.

All but Smarty. He waited till they were out of sight, then he laughed. He began to pick up the dropped goods and stuff them into a big sack.

'How foolish they are!' he said. 'They rush off and leave all their goods to me – and there isn't a wizard for miles around.'

Then a deep voice spoke from the nearby cave and made him jump.

'Smarty! Come here! Bring those goods to me!'

Smarty went pale and jumped. Who was that? 'Who are you?' he stammered.

'Well, you told the others,' said the deep voice. 'Who used to live here, Smarty? Why, the wizard of Woolamalooloo! Bring those goods to me, Smarty – and all your own goods too!'

Smarty wailed in fright. Oh, oh, to think the real wizard was there, after all! What a piece of bad luck. Shaking with fright, he took everything to the cave and threw it down outside. He could not see inside because it was far too dark.

'Leave the goods there,' said the deep voice. 'And come inside, Smarty. Come inside and see what happens to nasty little brownies like you. Come inside, Smarty.'

But Smarty didn't. He fled over the hill, back to the market, through the town there and out to the land of Far-Off-and-Forgotten. Never, never would he go back to Whispering Wood again!

The wizard in the cave chuckled as he saw Smarty

tearing away. He came out – and dear me, what was this? He was no wizard! He was just Stouty the brownie, not even dressed up! He picked up the sack of goods and went down the hill to the town, laughing loudly.

The other brownies gathered round him eagerly. 'Stouty – how did you get our goods? Oh, Stouty, did you see the wizard? Stouty, weren't you afraid of him?'

'No,' said Stouty with another laugh. 'Why, he lost all his magic powers one day and went to work for my great-granny – and he's there still, digging her garden and weeding and watering all day long. The wizard of Woolamalooloo indeed! Why, we call him Woolly for short, and he wouldn't hurt a fly!'

'You're better than any wizard, Stouty!' said his friends. 'We guess Smarty won't come back here any more!'

He won't. He's much too afraid of the wizard who wasn't there!

Mr
Grumble-Grumps

Mr Grumble-Grumps

OLD MR Grumble-Grumps was just as cross as his name, and nobody took much notice of him until a most surprising thing happened to him one day.

A small magical brownie came to live with him! Now this seems an extraordinary thing – but, you see, Mr Grumble-Grumps didn't believe in fairies, and so, of course, he couldn't see one, even if one was there! Because, as you know, what you don't believe in, you can never see.

So this brownie was quite safe with Mr Grumble-Grumps, because the old fellow could never see him. So the brownie had a very fine time. He sat on the table when Mr Grumble-Grumps ate his meals, and helped himself off the old chap's plate. He took sugar lumps out of the basin at teatime. He sipped Mr Grumble-Grumps's cocoa at suppertime. Grumble-Grumps did sometimes wonder how it was that his gravy seemed to disappear so quickly, and his sugar to vanish and his cocoa to go – but he couldn't see anyone taking them, so he just shook his head and thought no more of it.

The brownie got very bold. One day he was sitting half asleep on the peak of Grumble-Grumps's old cloth cap. The old man wanted to go out, so he picked up his cap and put it on. He didn't see the brownie there. The little fellow thought it would be rather fun to go out and see the world, sitting on Mr Grumble-Grumps's cap. But he forgot that other people could see him if they believed in fairies!

Mr Grumble-Grumps went out into the village. Soon he met Susie, the baker's daughter. When she saw the brownie sitting cheekily on the peak of his cap, she stared and stared and stared.

'What are you staring at, rude little girl?' said Mr Grumble-Grumps.

'You've got a fairy sitting on your cap,' said Susie.

'Bah! You're a little storyteller!' said the old man crossly and went on his way. Soon he met little Mrs Dimple. She believed in fairies, and she saw the brownie sitting on the peak of the cap. So she stared too, in the greatest surprise.

'Is anything the matter with my head this morning, Mrs Dimple?' asked Grumble-Grumps in a cross sort of voice.

'Not exactly,' said Mrs Dimple, 'but it's so funny, you've got a fairy sitting on your cap!'

'Pooh! How many more sillies am I going to meet this morning?' said Grumble-Grumps angrily. He snatched off his cap – but, of course, *he* couldn't see the brownie! The tiny fellow nearly fell to the ground. He just managed to cling on to one of Mr Grumble-Grumps's buttons, on the front of his coat.

There he stayed, though the old man didn't know, of course.

But soon he met George, the sweep's little boy. George stared at the brownie as if he couldn't believe his eyes. It was the first one he had ever seen.

'What in the world are you staring at my buttons for?' said old Mr Grumble-Grumps, beginning to feel quite uncomfortable.

'You've got a fairy hanging on to one of your buttons,' said George with a giggle. 'You do look funny!'

'Bah!' said Mr Grumble-Grumps, and he went on his way with such a frown that poor George sped home in a great hurry.

Before long the old fellow met a young man who wrote poetry. He happened to believe in fairies too, for most poets do – and when he saw the brownie hanging on to Mr Grumble-Grumps's button, he stopped and smiled in delight.

'And what are *you* staring and grinning at my chest

for?' said Mr Grumble-Grumps, beginning to think that everyone must have gone quite mad.

'I say! Don't you know what you've got?' said the poet. 'You've got a fairy hanging on to your button! Oh, don't look so cross – don't go – let me see it more closely!'

But Mr Grumble-Grumps wouldn't stop. He felt more annoyed than ever. He brushed away at his button and the brownie fell down on to his boot. There he held on tightly, for he did not want to lose Mr Grumble-Grumps! He wanted to go back home with him again, and the easiest way was to hang on to his boot and let him walk him back!

Soon the old fellow met little Lucy, the cobbler's daughter. She caught sight of the brownie clinging to Mr Grumble-Grumps's boot and she laughed in delight. She stared and stared down at the boot and Mr Grumble-Grumps shouted at her, 'Whatever are you staring at? Aren't my boots clean enough for you? Or perhaps you haven't seen boots before?'

'Oh yes, I have,' said Lucy. 'But you've got a fairy on your boot, Mr Grumble-Grumps!'

Grumble-Grumps looked down – but of course he couldn't see the brownie, for he didn't believe in them. So he saw nothing and, muttering angrily that people were playing silly jokes that day, he marched off again, with the brownie going up and down, up and down as he walked!

Then he met little Miss Twinkle, and she saw the brownie at once. She was so surprised to see one on old Grumble-Grumps's boot that she stared in astonishment. Mr Grumble-Grumps stared back at her. He liked Miss Twinkle. She was always so kind and so sweet, even to him.

'I suppose, Miss Twinkle,' he said, 'you are going to say there's a fairy on my boot! Everyone has been playing that silly joke on me this morning. I'm getting tired of it. I didn't think *you* would tell me a silly story like that.'

'Oh, Mr Grumble-Grumps, do you think it is a

joke and a story?' said Miss Twinkle. 'It's quite true –
there *is* a fairy on your boot. You are very lucky. Can't
you really see it? How sorry I am for you if you can't
see a thing like that!'

Mr Grumble-Grumps looked down at his boot.
No – he couldn't see that brownie. He didn't say
anything but he went home and thought hard, while
the brownie went to the bag of cakes and nibbled a
bit of sugar off the top of one.

'I can't see that fairy because I don't believe in
things like that,' said Grumble-Grumps. 'But it's a
strange thing if those people that *do* believe in them –
like little Lucy and that boy George – and Miss
Twinkle – do see them and say so! Suppose one
really is there – suppose he would give me a wish? I'll
believe in him! I will, I really will! Now, where is he?'

He looked round and saw the brownie nibbling
the sugar off the cake – but as soon as the brownie
saw Mr Grumble-Grumps looking at him, and knew
that he saw him, he jumped down from the table,

rushed to the door and slipped out!

'Come back!' yelled old Grumble-Grumps. 'I believe in you! I can see you! Come back!'

The brownie popped his sly little head round the door. 'You only believed in me because you thought you would get a wish!' he cried. 'I'm off somewhere else! You may believe in me all you like – but you won't get me living with you when you know I'm here, because you'd soon be horrid to me. I am only safe with you just so long as you don't know I'm here! Goodbye!'

And that was the last that Grumble-Grumps saw of the brownie. He was so cross about it that he stopped believing in fairies at once – so now he doesn't know if the brownie has come back to live with him again or not. I hope I meet him with the fairy sitting on his cap, don't you? I *should* laugh!

The Sticky Gnome's Prank

The Sticky Gnome's Prank

THE STICKY gnome walked along the little path that ran over Bumble Bee Common, humming a merry tune. It was a fine sunny day and he felt happy. In his left hand he carried his pot of brown glue and under his right arm were three brushes.

Sticky went about gluing broken things for people. His glue was very strong and could mend things and make them as good as new. He made it himself and he was very proud of it.

Now as he went along the little grassy path he saw a pair of shoes and a top hat lying beside a gorse bush. He was surprised to see them there and he looked about to see whose they were. And on the other side of the bush, he saw a gnome lying down fast asleep.

Sticky stood looking at him, wondering who he was. He was dressed in a blue silk coat and bright-yellow trousers, so he looked very smart.

As Sticky looked at the sleeping gnome a naughty thought came into his head, and he grinned a wicked grin. He dipped one of his brushes into his pot of glue and stirred it round until it was covered with the sticky mess. Then he carefully painted the rim of each empty shoe, and, turning up the top hat, he painted the inside of that too! Then he stood back and laughed to himself. There stood the gnome's shoes side by side, and there was the top hat – all neatly brushed with the stickiest glue in the whole kingdom.

Now I must wake him up and see him put them on! thought Sticky, chuckling. So he went behind the bush and shouted as loudly as ever he could, 'Hey! Hey! Hey!'

The sleeping gnome woke up with a jump and sat

up in a hurry. He looked all round to see where the shouting had come from.

'I wonder what woke me,' he said. 'I am sure I heard someone shouting. What's the time? Dear, oh, dear, it's already twelve o'clock! I shall never be in time to meet the dear prince!'

With that he slipped on his shoes as quickly as he could and put his top hat firmly on his head. How the naughty sticky gnome chuckled to himself to see him!

'I'll follow him and see what happens when he tries to take off his hat,' said Sticky. So he followed the gnome as closely as he could without being seen. He soon saw that the gnome was going to the station to meet the prince he had spoken of.

'Then he'll have to take off his hat, and he won't be able to,' said the wicked little gnome, dancing in delight to think of the naughty trick he had played. Now on the way to the station the gnome got a stone in one of his shoes. So, of course, he bent down to take it off so that he might shake out the stone. And then, to his enormous astonishment, he found that he couldn't pull the shoe from his foot. It stuck there as tightly as could be!

The gnome pulled and tugged at it. No use at all! The shoe wouldn't move at all.

'Extraordinary!' said the gnome in amazement. 'What's the matter with it? It's never been like this before. I'll try the other shoe and see if that will come off.'

But of course it wouldn't. It was stuck as tightly as the other one. The poor gnome was in an awful state about it. He looked at his watch and found that it was really getting very late indeed. He would have to go to the station as fast as ever he could. So off he hobbled, limping badly because the stone hurt him. Sticky followed, keeping out of sight, for he felt sure that the gnome would be very angry with him if he guessed what had happened.

The train was in the station when the gnome got

there. The prince was looking all round and he was annoyed not to see anyone to meet him. As soon as he saw the gnome he went up to him and shook him by the hand – and, to the prince's great surprise, the gnome didn't take off his top hat to him!

The poor gnome certainly tried to – but his hat was stuck as tightly as his shoes and he couldn't lift it at all. It was most alarming.

'Why don't you take off your hat when you greet me?' the prince asked crossly.

'I'm really very sorry,' said the poor gnome, as red as a tomato, 'but I can't seem to get it off.'

'Then you should wear a larger size,' snapped the prince. 'Come along, let's walk to your house. I don't want to ride. It's such a nice walk over Bumble Bee Common.'

So off they went together, the prince and the gnome. But the gnome still had a stone in his left shoe and he limped very badly.

'What's the matter with your foot?' asked the

prince, quite annoyed to find the gnome hobbling along so slowly.

'There's a stone in one of my shoes,' said the gnome humbly. 'I'm very sorry.'

'Well, take it out then!' said the prince.

'I can't,' said the gnome. 'My shoes are stuck as hard as my hat. I'm so sorry, Prince – but I can't really think what has happened.'

'Perhaps it's a spell,' said the prince, and he knelt down to look at the gnome's shoes. He pushed a finger into one and looked up at the gnome.

'Someone's played a trick on you,' he said. 'There is glue inside your shoes – and very strong, sticky glue it is too! Let me put my finger under your hat – yes, that's sticky too! Dear, dear, who's been playing pranks on you, I'd like to know?'

The sticky gnome was chuckling to see all that was happening – he had hidden behind a bush and was peeping out to see. But he didn't know that the prince was a powerful enchanter! Before half a minute had passed the prince had called out a string of magic words to bring before him the one who had played such a wicked prank on the poor gnome – and to Sticky's fright and alarm he found himself being forced to run right up to the prince and the gnome, taking his glue and all of his brushes with him!

'Oho! So you're the one who has done this, are you?' said the prince, peering into the pot and seeing the glue there. 'Come here!'

He took hold of Sticky, dipped a brush in the glue pot and began pasting him with the glue from head to foot! Sticky – and he really was very sticky now – howled dismally. The gnome looked on in astonishment. Then he rolled up his sleeves and said, 'Let me have a turn, Prince! I'd like to do a bit of pasting too. There's more than one brush, and I will make him beg to be let off and promise never to be naughty again!'

But when Sticky saw the gnome dip another brush into the glue pot, he was frightened and fled away as fast as ever he could, with his pot of glue and his brushes. The gnome ran after him for a long way and only gave up the chase when he saw Sticky running through the gates of Fairyland and into our world.

Sticky is still with us – do you know what he does? He paints all the chestnut buds with glue and makes the lime trees sticky in the summer. He gives some of his glue to the spiders for their webs – so it's no wonder they are so sticky, is it? Perhaps you will see him some day if you keep a sharp lookout.

'Hallo! How Are You?'

THE THREE cousins were staying with their Auntie Meg. There were Julian and his sister Anne, and Alice, their cousin.

It was fun at Auntie Meg's, because she had an enormous garden with a little wood at the end, a pond in a corner with ducks, and a big hen run. There were trees to climb, eggs to collect each day and fruit to pick.

Auntie Meg made a few rules about the garden. 'First, you may *not* help yourself to the peaches in the greenhouse,' she said. 'Nor must you go and take more than two tomatoes each in a day. Do *not* throw sticks or stones up into the big plum tree to get down plums, but wait until the gardener can pick them for you. Those are the three rules you must keep.'

'All right, Auntie,' said Julian at once. 'What *may* we pick?'

'Any other fruit,' said Auntie. 'The ripe gooseberries, the raspberries, the little wild strawberries in our tiny wood – and you may also pick pods of peas for yourselves, but please ask the gardener which row.'

No wonder it was fun to stay with Auntie Meg! It was grand to wander round the garden and pull a dozen golden yellow gooseberries off the laden bushes and then go to the raspberry canes and pick a handful of ripe red berries there. It was fun to take a few long green pods full of peas and climb one of the trees and sit there to have a feast!

But Alice longed for the peaches most of all! She stood outside the greenhouse and gazed in at the delicious velvety peaches a dozen times a day.

Gardener saw her and called out, 'Now don't you go in there, missy. And don't you take more than your share of tomatoes! I've missed more than I should the last two days.'

'I only take two tomatoes, like the others,' said Alice at once. 'And I haven't even *touched* a peach!'

The peaches and tomatoes were grown in the same greenhouse, but a glass partition and a door divided it into two. In the first half were the tomato plants, already hung with ripe red fruit, warm and smooth to the touch. In the further half were the peaches. Alice always wished she could slip through the glass dividing door and pick one of the reddest, biggest peaches!

'Do you know, Alice is a fibber, Anne,' said Julian to his sister that evening. 'She says she takes only two tomatoes, just as we do – but she takes far more! She waits till Gardener goes to feed the hens, then she slips into the greenhouse and picks some more.'

'Did you see her?' said Anne, shocked. 'Where does she put the tomatoes then? I never see her eating more than two.'

'Oh, I expect she's got a hidey-hole somewhere,' said Julian. 'Let's slip away this evening when we go to help to feed the hens, and see what Alice is doing. She never comes to help with the hens now.'

So they slipped away – and were just in time to see Alice coming out of the greenhouse with a handful of tomatoes – and a big peach!

'*Alice!*' said Julian. 'You know what Auntie Meg said.'

'Are you going to tell tales?' asked Alice, looking fierce. 'You always say you never tell tales.'

Julian hesitated. 'Well – I won't tell tales if you promise not to be so mean,' he said. 'We did promise Auntie, you know – *you* promised too.'

'Well, what does it matter, taking a few extra tomatoes and one peach?' said Alice. 'There are plenty.'

'Breaking a promise matters a lot,' said Anne.

'*That's* what matters! We shan't tell tales, you know that. But Gardener will, if he sees you!'

Alice made a face and disappeared down to the end of the garden. The others did not follow her. 'Gone to eat them or hide them, I suppose,' said Julian in disgust. 'Let's go back to the hens.'

'Julian, do you suppose Alice took the two jam tarts that Auntie's cook said were missing yesterday?' said Anne.

'Quite likely,' said Julian. 'People who take one thing will take another. Well, all I hope is that *we* don't get the blame!'

Alice was quite sure that her two cousins would not tell tales of her – but all the same she made up her mind to be more careful, and not to let *any*one see her when she raided the larder, took any of Auntie's chocolates or went to get a peach or extra tomatoes. She had even thrown sticks up into the big plum tree to bring down the ripe fruit – but Gardener began to make such a fuss when he found sticks about that Alice decided it wasn't safe to go on with *that* little game!

One afternoon Julian and Anne went out with their aunt. Alice said it was too hot and she was tired. 'I'll just stay quietly and read a book,' she said. Julian looked at Anne. They both guessed that Alice meant to do a little more raiding when she was alone! Horrid Alice! What was she going after now – peaches? Plums? Tomatoes?

Alice was after the peaches. She had seen that a great many were ripe now, for the sun was hot. She was sure that she could take at least six without anyone noticing they were gone.

Then what a feast I'll have! she thought.

So when everyone was safely out of the way, and Gardener was tidying up the potting shed, she stole down to the big greenhouse and went inside. She had to go through the rows of tomatoes before she came to the peaches. She opened the glass door in the middle of the greenhouse and tiptoed in – oh, the wonderful peaches!

And then she jumped almost out of her skin.

'Hallo!' said a voice. 'How are you? Nice day, isn't it?'

Alice trembled and her knees shook. She stared all round, but she couldn't see anyone at all. Who was it?

'HALLO!' said the voice more loudly, and Alice turned and fled! Oh, what a horrid voice it was! And there was nobody there – what did it mean?

She ran indoors and hid in her bedroom. She was really very frightened. *Who* had been in the peach house – and where had he hidden? There wasn't anywhere to hide! She sat on her bed and wondered for a long time.

After a bit she got up. 'I must have *imagined* it!' she said to herself. 'How silly of me! Perhaps the sun has been too hot today and I've got a tiny bit of sunstroke. Yes – I just imagined it! All the same, I shan't go into the peach house again!'

But, will you believe it, when Julian and Anne went

with Gardener to feed the hens that evening, Alice crept off to the greenhouse to get some tomatoes! *I won't go into the part where the peaches grow – only just inside the tomato half*, she thought. *And all I need to do is to put my hand inside and pick a few tomatoes off the first plant – I don't even need to step right inside!*

Julian saw Alice slipping off and nudged Anne. 'I bet she's off to the tomato house,' he said. 'She had her two tomatoes already this morning – and I expect she had plenty when we were out this afternoon!'

Alice picked one tomato, and was just about to pick another, when she heard the voice again.

'Hallo! How are you?'

Alice dropped the tomatoes, gave a scream and fled down the garden to her two cousins. She was so frightened that she felt she really must be with somebody. That awful voice again! And yet there was nobody there – Alice had taken a quick look round the rows of tomatoes, but there really was *nobody* there, nobody at all. Anyway, who would be small enough to hide behind tomato plants?

'What's the matter, Alice?' asked Julian, wondering at her pale face and her shaking knees.

'Nothing,' said Alice. But then tears came into her eyes and she gave a sudden sob. Anne took her arm and led her out of Gardener's hearing.

'What's up?' she asked. 'You look strange, Alice!'

'Oh – I'll *have* to tell you – I'm so very frightened!' said poor Alice, and out came the whole story of the strange voice in the peach house – and again in the tomato house. 'But there was NOBODY there!' wailed Alice.

'Strange voices – and nobody there – impossible!' said Julian, laughing. 'You be careful not to go and take buns or tarts out of the larder again, Alice – the voice might be there too!'

'She's *really* frightened, Julian,' said Anne. 'Don't laugh at her. Alice, come indoors with me. Have a drink of water or something – you'll feel better then.'

She led Alice away, but Julian did not go with

them. He didn't believe a word of Alice's story! He went off to the greenhouse himself and walked inside. And at once a voice spoke to him.

'Hallo! How are you?'

Julian jumped in fright. Good gracious – there *was* a voice then? He looked all round, but could see no one.

'Who are you?' he said in rather a shaky voice.

'Nice day, isn't it?' said the voice at once, and then Julian saw something moving behind a thick tomato plant. Very bravely he went up to it and peered cautiously round.

Two bright eyes looked into his. 'Hallo! How are you?' said the voice again – but this time Julian saw who it belonged to!

'A parrot! A talking parrot! Well, you certainly scared Alice all right!' said Julian. 'And me too! You belong to Auntie's friend next door, don't you? I'll take you back.'

The parrot, pleased with the boy's friendly voice,

flew to his shoulder. 'How are you?' it said. 'Nice day, how are you?'

'I'm quite all right – and I'd like to know how many peaches and tomatoes you've eaten,' said Julian, going out of the greenhouse. 'Come along – it's time you were back home.'

The old lady next door was very pleased to see her parrot again. 'Oh, thank you!' she said to Julian. 'He's a naughty boy to fly away!'

'Naughty boy!' said the parrot solemnly. 'How are you?'

Julian laughed and went to find his sister. He took her into a corner and told her what had happened. She laughed out loud.

'Oh! How funny! Just a parrot hiding there after all! Oh, Julian – Alice is quite certain that there is somebody watching her now, whenever she goes to take things that she shouldn't. She says she daren't even go into the larder now, or into the cupboard where Auntie keeps the chocolates and biscuits.

Whatever will she say when you tell her it was only a parrot?'

The Disappearing Hats

The Disappearing Hats

ONCE UPON a time, in the village of Get-About, there was a hat shop. Two gnomes owned it, Sniffle and Snuffle. They made excellent top hats in all colours – blue, pink, yellow and green, for the folk of Get-About went to a great many meetings and parties, and wore top hats very often.

And then a strange thing happened. The top hats belonging to the people of Get-About began to disappear in a very peculiar way!

Burly-One the gnome had just bought a magnificent green one with a yellow band round it. He wore it to a meeting in the next village and felt very smart indeed.

He came home and hung it up as usual in the hall. The next day it wasn't there!

Then another hat disappeared. This time it was Curly-Top's hat. He was a pixie and had a very choice top hat – pink with a blue band, and he had stuck a little feather in at the side. He had put his in a box on a shelf in his bedroom – but bless us all, when he looked in the box the next day, the hat was gone! The only thing in the box was the little feather.

When Curly-Top and Burly-One met and began to tell one another about their vanished hats, two others came up and said theirs had gone too!

'I put mine on the kitchen table,' said Bong the magical brownie. 'And this morning it wasn't there.'

'And I put mine on the knob at the end of my bed,' said Chortle the elf. 'And I know it was there when I went to sleep, because my wife said to me, "Chortle, you've put your hat on the knob again instead of in its box." So I know it was there – and this morning it was gone!'

'And there's the party today at Lord High-and-Mighty's,' groaned Burly-One. 'What are we to do?' We *must* go in top hats!'

'We'd better go to Sniffle and Snuffle and see if they have any hats to fit us,' said Curly-Top. 'I don't expect they will have.'

They went to the gnomes' shop and explained to them about their vanished hats. Sniffle and Snuffle listened and looked very surprised indeed.

'Now the thing is, Sniffle and Snuffle,' said Bong, 'we've got this party this afternoon. Can you possibly let us have top hats in time?'

'I suppose you'd like them just the same as your others?' said Sniffle.

'Yes,' said everyone.

'Well, we'll try to manage them in time,' said Sniffle. 'But we are afraid we will have to charge you more than usual, as we shall have to work so hard.'

'Oh, dear!' groaned Chortle. 'Well, I suppose it can't be helped.'

Exactly ten minutes before Curly-Top, Burly-One, Chortle and Bong were ready to set off to their party, their hats arrived from Sniffle and Snuffle. They each put them on in delight. Really, they might have been the same hats they had lost! They fitted perfectly.

Now that night three other hats disappeared belonging to Fee, Fi and Fo, three brother goblins. They were terribly upset because they had to go to a most important meeting that day – and how could they be seen out without their fine top hats?

'I put mine in my bedroom on the top of the wardrobe,' said Fee.

'And I hung mine on the chair,' said Fi.

'I don't know where I put mine, but it was *some*where!' groaned Fo.

'We'd better go to Sniffle and Snuffle and see if they can let us have hats in time,' said Fee. So off they went – and the two gnomes promised to work hard and send three hats in good time.

'But we shall have to charge you more money,' said Sniffle.

Now as more and more top hats disappeared the people of Get-About village became very angry. They lay in wait for the robbers who they thought must come to steal their hats – but never a robber did they see! It was all most peculiar.

The only people who didn't mind about the disappearing hats were Sniffle and Snuffle, who did a roaring trade and charged everyone more than usual because they were so busy and had to work so hard.

At last Fee, Fi and Fo, whose hats had disappeared for the second time, went to visit the wise woman, Dame Thinkitout. She listened to their tale and then nodded her head. 'So you want to find the thieves?' she said. 'Well, tie a long, long string to your hats, goblins, and then, when they disappear, follow the string and you'll find the thieves at the end of it!'

'What a good idea!' said Fee, Fi and Fo. They went home and each of them carefully tied a very,

very long string to their hat. One end was round the hat and the other was tied tightly to the bed knob.

Nothing happened that night – but the next night the goblins were awakened by a strange whistling sound. They lit a candle. Their hats were gone!

'Quick!' said Fee, tumbling out of bed. 'We must follow the strings!'

They found that the strings went out of the window – down the garden, across the road, over the long meadow, down the hill – and into – where do you think? Why, into Sniffle and Snuffle's shop! Yes, really!

The goblins peeped into the shop through a crack in the curtain. They saw Sniffle and Snuffle there. Sniffle was standing in the middle of the room, chanting a magic rhyme, and Snuffle was standing with his arms out to catch the hats that came in at the window!

'Oh! The wicked robbers!' said Fee, Fi and Fo angrily. 'They make our top hats – and put a disappearing spell in them so that they can get them back – and then sell them to us again for more money than before!'

The goblins all climbed in at the window and began to shout at the surprised gnomes.

'Robbers! Thieves! Wait till the people of Get-About hear what we've found out! Yes – just wait till tomorrow morning!'

'Mercy, mercy!' begged the two gnomes, pale with fright.

'Certainly not!' said Fee, and pinched Sniffle's long nose. He had wanted to do that for a long time. 'Give us our hats!'

The goblins took their hats, put them on and stalked out of the shop. 'Aha! You wait till tomorrow!' said Fo.

You can guess how angry the folk of Get-About were when they heard all that Fee, Fi and Fo had to tell them. They marched to the gnomes' shop next morning – but it was closed! A notice hung outside.

GONE AWAY.

YOU CAN ALL EAT YOUR HATS!

'What cheek!' snorted Chortle in a rage.

'Well, we can at any rate use the hats they've had to leave behind!' said Bong. There were heaps of top hats in the shop. The folk of Get-About tried them on. There were enough for everyone to have two or three.

'I'm glad I pulled Sniffle's long nose last night,' said Fee. 'I wish I had pulled Snuffle's too!'

Nobody knows what became of the two bad gnomes – and a very good thing too!

The Wizard's Watering Can

The Wizard's Watering Can

IT WAS very hot weather. Daddy's garden was dry and brown. The grass was fading and the plants were drooping. Daddy went out to look at his roses and he shook his head sadly.

'Dear me!' he said. 'Look at this! The garden won't have a single flower or blade of grass soon, if some watering isn't done. Polly! Bobby! Come here a minute. I want you.'

Polly and Bobby stopped their game of hide-and-seek and ran to their daddy.

'I want you to do some watering for me, my dears,' said Daddy. 'You have each got a watering can, haven't you? Well, you must water the garden for me this evening, and every evening until the rain comes. You can do that quite well.'

'Oh, Daddy! Billy and Peter come to play with us in the evenings,' said Bobby. 'Need we water the garden?'

'You'll do as you're told,' said Daddy. 'Billy and Peter can help you or can stay away, just as you choose. But the garden must be watered.'

The children were cross. They didn't want to water the garden. It took such a long time. They were so sulky and cross that Mummy got tired of them at home that afternoon and told them to go for a walk. So off they went.

'Let's go to the woods where it's cool,' said Polly. So they took the little narrow path that led between the hazel trees in Wizard Wood. It was a big wood, very thick in the centre. The children had often wondered why it was called Wizard Wood, but nobody knew.

'I expect once upon a time a wizard really lived

here,' said Polly as they ran through the cool wood. 'Oh, I wish we could see him, don't you, Bobby!'

'Pooh! Wizards don't belong to nowadays,' said Bobby scornfully. 'Where are you going, Polly? We've never been as far as this before!'

'I'm just exploring!' said Polly. 'Look, this funny little path must lead to somewhere. I'm sure it's not a bunny path.'

They walked on in the shade of the whispering trees. The sunlight crept through the leaves here and there and lay in twinkling golden freckles on the ground. Polly went on and on, and at last the trees were so thick that not even a spot of sunshine could get through them.

And then the children suddenly saw a funny little house. It was very small, very crooked and very strange. It stood in a small clearing and the sunshine poured down on it. Round it was a garden in which grew the largest, most brilliant flowers that Polly and Bobby had ever seen. They were as large as dinner plates and were all colours of the rainbow. They shone like jewels and the two children stopped in surprise.

As they stared at the bright garden they saw the door of the cottage open. A small man came out in an old shabby tunic. He wore on his head a tall hat with a peacock's feather stuck in it. His shoes were green and had long pointed toes.

'It's the wizard!' whispered Polly, clutching hold of Bobby's arm in excitement. 'Fancy! He lives here still, right in the heart of the wood!'

As the children watched they saw the old man take a watering can from a hook on the wall. It was a large can, painted yellow and blue. The wizard filled it with water from the well at the end of his garden, and then he stood it on the ground and spoke to it.

'Watering can, do your work today,
And water my garden as well as you may!'

THE WIZARD'S WATERING CAN

That is what the children heard the wizard say, and at once the can rose up in the air, tilted itself and began to water the strange, brilliant flowers. It never seemed to get empty, but passed on from one plant to another, giving each a good soaking. Then it watered the little patch of grass very thoroughly. After that it watered some plants in a tub.

The wizard had gone indoors, so the children moved closer to watch the strange watering can. When the door opened and the wizard again appeared Polly and Bobby ran back into the wood, afraid of being seen. After a while they peeped out. The door of the cottage was shut, the wizard was gone and the watering can hung quietly up on its hook on the wall.

Presently the children heard a door bang and they saw the wizard walking down a path at the back of the house. He had gone out of his back door to do some shopping, for he carried a big basket on his arm.

'Bobby! Let's borrow that wonderful watering can and water Daddy's garden tonight!' said Polly suddenly. 'We can take it from its hook, carry it home and bring it back as soon as it has done all the watering. Then we can still have Peter and Billy to play and we needn't any of us bother about the watering. The can will do it all! We can take it back when it has finished.'

'Ooh, do you think the wizard will mind?' said Bobby. 'Suppose he missed it?'

'Oh, don't keep supposing things,' cried Polly impatiently. 'You're always afraid to do things. *I'll* get the can!'

She ran into the wizard's garden, took the can from the hook and ran back again, red with excitement. Then they made their way home. They hid the can in the gardener's shed and went to have their tea.

'Don't forget that Daddy told you to water the garden thoroughly tonight,' said Mummy, when they left the table.

'No, Mummy,' said Polly, and out they went. Soon Billy and Peter came, and the two children showed their friends the magic watering can.

'Daddy said we were to water the garden instead of playing with you,' said Polly. 'But we've borrowed this magic can, and it will do all the work for us, and we'll play with you while it does it!'

Billy and Peter could hardly believe their ears. Polly filled the can with water from the tap and then set it on the ground as she had seen the wizard do.

'Watering can, do your work today,
And water my garden as well as you may!'

she said in a loud voice.

At once the can rose up, tilted itself and began to water the flowers in the beds very thoroughly. It didn't get empty at all – it just went on and on watering, moving from plant to plant in a very marvellous way.

The children were delighted. What an easy way to water the garden! Soon they were tired of watching the hard-working can and ran to play their favourite game of hide-and-seek.

After a little while the can stopped watering the beds and began to soak the grass. When it had finished that it seemed to look round for something else to water. But there were no more flowers at all. So the can moved to Polly's dolls' pram and began to water that!

Polly saw it and gave a scream.

'Oh! The wizard's can is watering my dolls' pram! Oh, the dolls are all wet and the pram cover is dripping!'

She ran to stop the can from watering her pram any more, but to her surprise, as soon as she tried to get hold of the can it turned the spout towards her and watered *her*!

She ran off with a shout of anger. Then the three boys tried to get hold of the can, but it did just the same to them. It gave them all a good drenching and they had to give up.

'Stop the horrid thing watering any more,' said Billy, squeezing the water from his shirt. 'Why don't you say the words that stop it, Polly? You started it, didn't you?'

But Polly didn't know how to stop the can from watering. She hadn't heard or seen what the wizard did to stop it. She turned pale and stood still.

'Bobby, what shall we do? We don't know how to stop the can. It will go on and on watering everything, and we can't even get hold of it to take it back to the wizard.'

'Well, it's all your silly fault!' said Bobby. '*You* wanted to borrow the can. I didn't think we ought to. But you always *will* do silly, naughty things and get us into trouble. I'm sure *I* don't know what we'll do!'

'Well, *we're* going home!' said Billy, taking Peter's hand. 'We're wet through, all because of your silly wizard's can, and we shall get into trouble. Goodbye!'

The two boys ran off and left Bobby and Polly with the magic watering can. It was still watering! It had gone to Bobby's wooden horse and was watering that!

Then it went to the hammock Mummy sometimes

rested in and began to water that. Polly ran to it, for she knew that Mummy would be very cross to find her hammock wet – but the can simply turned its spout on her and watered her from head to foot. Polly burst out crying, but it wasn't a bit of good. The can took no notice at all, and just went on watering everything.

It watered the dog's kennel. It watered the dustbin. It soaked all the clothes that Jane the housemaid had hung out on the line to dry. It even poked its spout in at the nursery window and watered the curtains there! Bobby began to feel very frightened. What would Daddy say when he came home?

'Perhaps Daddy will be able to stop the can when he comes!' said Bobby to Polly.

The can went to the garden seat and watered it up and down till it dripped and ran with silvery water. And just then the children heard Daddy coming home! They heard his car stopping outside and his voice greeting Mummy.

'Now Daddy will stop the horrid, hateful can!'

wept Polly. But, oh my goodness me, as soon as that wizard can heard Daddy coming, what do you think it did? Why, it shot straight up into the air and vanished like smoke! It had gone back to the wizard in the wood!

So when Daddy came out into the garden, all he could see was everything dripping wet, and two frightened, soaking-wet children. He stared round at the dripping garden seat, Mummy's wet hammock, the soaking clothes on the line, the drenched children. And he looked as dark as thunder!

'WHAT'S ALL THIS?' he asked in his biggest voice. 'How dare you water everything like this?'

Well, Bobby and Polly explained how they had borrowed the wizard's can and how they hadn't been able to stop it from soaking everything – but, do you know, Daddy didn't believe a word of it! Not a single word!

'Don't tell me such a ridiculous story!' he said sharply. 'A wizard's can indeed. You're just making it all up to excuse your naughtiness. You shall be put straight to bed.'

And dear me, they *were* sent to bed. They cried and were very sorry for themselves indeed, but Daddy wasn't a bit sorry for them, nor was Mummy. They were both very cross and impatient.

'Well, it serves us right for taking something that belonged to someone else without asking if we might,' said Bobby at last. 'We shouldn't have done it.'

'I'm sorry, Bobby,' said Polly. 'I won't be so silly again. I know it was my fault. Perhaps we had better go and find that wizard tomorrow and say we are sorry for taking his can, and that we hope it came back all right.'

So the next day they set off to the wood again. But although they hunted and hunted, and followed one little path after another, they could NOT find that little crooked house in the heart of the wood. Wasn't it strange?

As for the magic watering can, it went back to the

wizard all right. It hung itself up on the hook and all that night it chuckled and laughed to itself when it thought of what it had done in the children's garden. You should just have heard it!

Nobbly-One the
Gnome

Nobbly-One the Gnome

NOBBLY-ONE THE gnome lived in Snowdrop Cottage, all by himself. He was a plump, twinkling little fellow, sharp as a needle and as poor as a church mouse.

Snowdrop Cottage didn't look much like a Snowdrop – or like snow either! It had once had clean, white-washed walls outside, shining brightly in the sun – but now it was dirty and grey. Nobbly-One really hadn't the money to buy the whitewash.

Soon the cottage was so dirty that people began to talk about it.

'What a disgusting place!' said Gobo the goblin,

as he passed.

'What a horrible cottage!' said Pippitty the pixie, going by with his nose in the air.

Of course the nobbly gnome heard them, and he went very red. *It's a nuisance*, he thought. I *don't like my cottage to be dirty outside – but what can I do? I've only just a little whitewash, not nearly enough to do all the wall – and it would look dreadful to paint one wall and not the others. The white wall would make the other walls look dirtier than ever! Ah, well! If folks paid me a bit more money I could buy more whitewash.*

But nobody would pay him any more money for the sweeping and the scrubbing he did, so his cottage stayed dirty. And then one day Nobbly-One had an idea. He sat and thought about it for a little while, and he made up his mind to try it.

'If my plan is good,' he said gleefully, 'I shall not only get more money for whitewash, but I shall get all the work done for nothing!'

The next morning was lovely and sunny.

Nobbly-One mixed what little whitewash he had and then went out into the garden. He had a great big brush, which he kept dipping into his pail of whitewash, and then slap-slap-slap, he slapped the whitewash on the wall. It was fun to do!

Now along the road came Criss-Cross the magical brownie, a frown on his face, for he was never in a very good temper. He stopped to watch Nobbly-One slapping the whitewash on his walls. The gnome was singing merrily.

'You sound very happy,' said Criss-Cross.

'So I am!' said Nobbly-One. 'Think what a fine job this is on a sunny morning! Slip-slap all the time, a nice messy job that makes you sing for joy!'

'I'd rather like to try it,' said Criss-Cross after a bit, simply longing to slap that big brush up and down the wall.

'Righto,' said Nobbly-One at once. 'A penny a time, because it's such a treat!'

Criss-Cross paid over his penny and took the

brush. Slip-slap! What fun! Dip in the bucket again! Slap-slap! Aha! That's the sort of job to take a frown away and make you sing! Slippitty-slap!

'You haven't much whitewash left,' said Criss-Cross. 'You'd better make some more. I'd like to finish this wall before I go. It's a treat to do this, I can tell you! How I envy you, Nobbly-One, having a whole cottage to do!'

Nobbly-One grinned to himself. He ran off to buy some more stuff to make whitewash with. When he came back he saw Binkie and Snippo, a pixie and an elf, standing watching Criss-Cross slapping on the whitewash.

'Hark at him singing!' said Binkie. 'I've never heard Criss-Cross sing before!'

'Hey, Nobbly-One,' said Snippo. 'Criss-Cross says you let him slap about for a penny. Will you let me have a turn too? It looks so lovely!'

'Yes, but what about me?' said Nobbly-One, pretending that he wanted to slap about himself. 'I've hardly had a turn yet.'

'We'll leave lots for you to do,' promised Snippo. 'Look here – I'll give you twopence if you'll let me have a turn now. Criss-Cross has just finished that wall.'

'And I'll give you twopence for a turn after Snippo's finished,' said Binkie eagerly. 'Ooh! Slippitty-slap! What a lovely thing to do on a sunny morning! What a mess we'll be in! Sloshity-slosh! Hark at that brush!'

'All right,' said Nobbly-One, turning away to hide a very wide grin indeed. 'You can each have a turn if you like. I'll take twopence a time.'

So Snippo and Binkie had turns at whitewashing the cottage, and you should have heard them singing at the job and slapping about with the brush! You should have seen the splashes of whitewash on their faces and clothes! My, they were as happy as blackbirds on a bright spring morning!

As for Nobbly-One, he rushed off with the

twopences and bought enough whitewash to finish his whole cottage! And he wore a grin that wouldn't come off.

It wasn't long before Hi-Ti the gnome came down the lane. Now Hi-Ti was a tailor and he sewed fine cloth with a little needle all day long – and when he saw the lovely slappitty-slaps of the big whitewash brush, so much larger than his tiny needles, he simply longed to have a turn too.

'Let me have a go, Nobbly-One,' he said to the little gnome.

'Twopence a time,' said the gnome at once. So Hi-Ti paid up a penny and two ha'pennies and stood impatiently waiting his turn. Snippo finished, and then Binkie finished – and at last it was Hi-Ti's turn.

You should have seen him! Ah, this was better than bending over a coat, sewing with a horrid little needle! He was out in the sunshine, making great slappitty-slaps up and down the wall, splashing himself from head to foot. What fun it was!

'Look at old Hi-Tiddly-Hi-Ti!' said Twinkle the pixie, coming up and looking over the wall. 'What-ho, Hi-Ti! You sound merry!'

'Ah, this is a lovely job!' said Hi-Ti happily. 'Does you all the good in the world! Criss-Cross has had a turn, so has Binkie, so has Snippo, and now it's my turn! Isn't Nobbly-One good to let us all have turns!'

Slippitty-slap went the brush, and Twinkle longed to have a turn too. It did look so nice. Slosh-slosh! Listen to that whitewash on the wall! How lovely to make such a dirty old wall so white and shining! Twinkle suddenly felt as if he *must* have a turn too!

'I say, Nobbly-One,' he said suddenly. 'Do let me have a turn as well. It looks fine.'

'No, I can't let you,' said Nobbly-One. 'There's only half a wall left to do, and I'm going to do that myself.'

'Oh, *do* let me,' said Twinkle earnestly. 'See, I'll give you threepence to let me finish it. Oh, *do*,

Nobbly-One, DO!'

'All right,' said the gnome, and he took the threepence with a very wide grin. Twinkle didn't notice the grin at all – he was too busy longing for Hi-Ti to finish his turn.

At last the little tailor had finished and Twinkle took up the brush. Slippitty-slap! Oh joy! How good it was to slosh about in the sunshine! Look at the dripping whitewash! How Twinkle enjoyed himself!

At last it was all finished. The cottage stood gleaming white, as good as new. How fine it looked! How everyone stared at it in admiration!

Nobbly-One sat down to a wonderful supper that night. Fried steak and onions and a big chocolate pudding to follow.

'It's the best meal I've had for months!' said the sly little gnome to himself. 'But I deserve it for my smartness. Ho ho! All my whitewash bought, and all my cottage painted for nothing – and fivepence in my moneybox at the end! Ho ho! There's nothing like making other people do your work and pay you for it too!'

Ah, Nobbly-One, you're too smart for anything! I'm glad *I* don't live in your village!

The Walking Bone

The Walking Bone

BONZO AND Benji were two puppies who lived in the park-keeper's cottage with Mr Tidy-Up, the park-keeper. Mr Tidy-Up's job was to plant out the flowers in the park, weed the flower beds, water them and, of course, to tidy up everything nicely. No crisp packets, no sweet bags, no bottles, no bits of paper were allowed to lie about on the grass or paths from one day to the next.

You might think that Bonzo and Benji would do their best to help their master, Mr Tidy-Up, for he was good to them, giving them bones and biscuits each day, and he had made a fine box for them with a little

283

rug inside. But no – the puppies were a terrible pair, untidy, lazy and mischievous.

The things they did! You wouldn't believe them! One day Mr Tidy-Up had very neatly labelled all the new plants in the big flower bed by the park gates – and those naughty pups rooted up the wooden labels as soon as his back was turned and chewed them all!

Another time they watched him planting the daffodil bulbs – and they thought they were some special kind of bones! So as soon as poor Mr Tidy-Up had gone to his tea the puppies dug up all the bulbs and bit them to see what they were like. Mr Tidy-Up gave them a good telling-off for that – but two days later they behaved just as badly as ever.

When they began to bury their bones all over the park beds, Mr Tidy-Up was cross.

'Now listen to me, Bonzo and Benji,' he said. 'I don't mind you burying your bones – but I WILL NOT HAVE you digging them up again! You've got such bad memories you don't remember where you put your bones, and you dig up half the park before you find anything. So just remember – bury your bones if you like – but DON'T DARE to dig them up again.'

Well, you might as well talk to the kettle on the stove as talk to Bonzo and Benji. They just didn't care for anyone. If they wanted to dig up bones, they would dig them up, so there!

'You know, Bonzo,' said Benji one sunny spring morning, 'I'd like to dig up that fine, juicy bone we stole from the butcher the other day. Where did we bury it? There was a nice lot of marrow in it we didn't have time to finish.'

'Didn't we bury it by the park gates, where the daffodils are?' said Bonzo.

'I don't think so,' said Benji. 'I think we buried it in the round flower bed by the duck pond.'

'Or was it in the bed of tulips?' asked Bonzo, thinking hard. 'Well – let's go and try in all those places.'

Off they went. They tried in the bed of yellow daffodils and dug up about fifty before they decided their bone was not there. Then off they went to the round flower bed by the duck pond, and after frightening two ducks nearly out of their lives, they dug up half the bed and then decided that they certainly hadn't buried the bone there at all.

'I say – did we put it by that old mossy wall over there?' said Benji suddenly. 'I seem to remember putting it there. Let's try there before we dig up the tulip bed.'

So off they went and dug hard in the wet bed at the foot of the old mossy wall. And they found something big and hard.

'It's our bone!' cried Bonzo, pleased. 'Look! Isn't it a big one! I'd forgotten it was so big, hadn't you, Benji? Let's take it to the woodshed and we can chew it there alone.'

So between them they carried the big, heavy thing to the woodshed and put it down on the floor. They lay down, panting, their little red tongues hanging out of their mouths.

They looked at the bone – and to their enormous surprise it moved! Yes, it did – it really did!

'Did you – did you see it move?' Bonzo asked Benji, very much afraid.

'I d-d-d-d-don't know,' said Benji, staring at the big brown thing in fright. It moved again.

'Ooooooh!' yelped Benji in a dreadful fright.

'It's got legs!' barked Bonzo, all the hair on his neck standing up in terror.

'And now it's grown a head!' yelped Benji, who was hardly able to stand up, he was so frightened.

It was quite true. The big bone had moved, put out four thick legs and then thrust out a head in which were two little eyes! It wasn't a bone, of course. It was a tortoise that had buried itself in the bed by the old mossy wall to sleep quietly through the winter. But the two puppies really did think it was a bone, and they were dreadfully frightened to think that their bone should grow a head and legs and look at them like that!

The tortoise wanted to get outside in the sunshine. It wanted to go and find a lettuce to eat. So it began to walk slowly towards the two puppies, meaning to go out of the door.

The dogs sprang up in fear. They yelped wildly and then, their tails between their legs, they fled out of the woodshed yelping, 'The bone's after us! The bone's after us!'

The tortoise was surprised to see the puppies behaving so strangely. But he was old and wise and nothing upset him. So he went quietly on his way to find a lettuce.

The puppies ran indoors and curled up together, shivering, in their cosy box.

'We have been very naughty dogs all our lives,' said Benji. 'This is a punishment to us. It is worse than anything.'

'Perhaps all our bones will come alive and grow

legs and heads,' said Bonzo, trembling as he remembered the tortoise putting out its little head and looking at him.

'I shan't be naughty any more,' said Benji. 'I shall be a good dog from now on.'

'And I'll never, ever go digging up bones or anything else as long as I live,' said Bonzo.

And from that day the puppies became two of the best dogs in the world – they were good, obedient, tidy and hard-working. Mr Tidy-Up doesn't know why and he is very much puzzled about it. I'd very much like to tell him about the Walking Bone, wouldn't you?

Goblin Magic

Goblin Magic

ONE DAY Hurry wanted some water from the well, because he was doing his washing and he needed to rinse it. So he called to Scurry, his friend.

'Hey, Scurry! Fetch me some water from the well, will you?'

'No, I won't,' said Scurry. 'Especially as you don't even say "please". Go and fetch it yourself.'

'Well, I will,' said Hurry in a temper, 'and what is more, I'll make you carry it, so there! Dinkle-um-ducket, change to a bucket. Dinkle-um-dell, off to the well!'

And hey presto, poor Scurry found himself

changing shape. His legs disappeared, so did his arms. He grew a thin, curved handle. He was a bucket!

He couldn't say a word, of course. He was just a pail to carry water in. Hurry grinned and picked up the pail by the handle.

'So you said you wouldn't go to the well and carry back water for me, did you?' he said. 'Well, you're going after all, and you'll come back carrying plenty of water for me to use. Ho, ho, ho!'

But halfway to the well Hurry met someone he didn't like at all. It was the goblin Crookity. Crookity called to Hurry, 'Hey! Always in a hurry, aren't you? Wait a bit, I want to talk to you.'

But Hurry wouldn't wait. He ran ahead as fast as he could, swinging the pail. Crookity ran after him.

'Hey! That's a funny pail you've got! Something strange about it, isn't there?' he cried.

'Yes, there is,' said Hurry fiercely. 'I've changed Scurry into this pail, see? So you be careful I don't change you into something.'

'You can't,' said Crookity. 'Nobody can. You know that. I'm too clever at magic for anyone to play a silly trick like that on me.'

Hurry knew that was true. Everyone was scared of Crookity because he knew so much magic. Nobody liked him, but nobody could get rid of him. Hurry scowled at him.

'You think you're so clever, do you? Well, you couldn't have changed Scurry into a bucket. I don't believe you could even change yourself into one!'

Clang! Crookity leapt high into the air and came down with a loud clang. He was a bucket, just like Scurry – without even a magic word either.

Then the strange little bucket giggled and leapt into the air. When it came down, it wasn't a bucket, it was Crookity again.

'Clever. Very clever,' said Hurry. 'I couldn't work magic as quickly as that. Can you change yourself into a – a broom, say?'

Swish! Crookity jumped high in the air and came

down again with a swish – but now he was a big broom, and dear me, he swept Hurry right off his feet so that he fell down with a bump. The broom laughed loudly, leapt into the air and there was Crookity again!

'That was very funny,' said Crookity, enjoying himself. 'What shall I turn into next?'

'Oh, dear. I don't know. Well – what about a – a – let me see – I can't think – well, what about a teapot?' said Hurry, getting scared.

Thud! Crookity leapt up into the air and came down with a thud. He was now a very large teapot, and out of the spout came a cloud of steam. And then, oh, dear, the teapot tilted itself and poured tea all over poor Hurry! He yelled and ran away, and the teapot bounced after him. But it laughed so much that it couldn't pour.

It leapt into the air, and when it came down again there was Crookity, rolling over and over on the ground, roaring with laughter at his joke. Hurry scowled at him. He picked up his pail. He had had enough of Crookity.

'No, no, you mustn't go,' said Crookity. 'Tell me something else. You say you want water in that bucket, which is really poor Scurry. Shall I change into water and fill the bucket – and then throw myself at you and drench you? Ho, ho, ho!'

Splash! He leapt into the air once more and came down in the bucket. He was now a lot of water that swirled round in the bucket. But before he could throw himself at Hurry and soak him from head to foot, Hurry caught up the bucket and ran to the well. He tipped up the full bucket – and down into the well went the water, *splishity*, *splashity*, *slishity*, *sloshity*!

Hurry leant over the well cautiously. Was the goblin powerful enough or clever enough to change back to his own shape again, now that he was in the well? Would he come clambering out, yelling and shouting?

The well water swirled and splashed, bubbled and

gurgled. Then it became quite calm, as it always was. No goblin appeared.

He's all mixed up with the well water! He can't find himself! He's split into different drops and he's got all mixed with the other drops, thought Hurry gleefully. *He's gone! We've got rid of him! Hurrah! Hurrah! I must go and tell Scurry.*

Then he remembered that Scurry was the bucket in his hand. He set it down and danced round it.

'Dinkle-um-ducket, no longer a bucket. Dinkle-um-durry, come back, dear Scurry!'

The bucket disappeared, and there was Scurry. The two flung themselves at one another. Hurry was almost crying.

'Oh, Scurry, dear Scurry, I'm sorry for what I did! Oh, Scurry, you carried Crookity, did you know?'

'Yes, I know – and you threw him down the well and he's gone, gone, *gone*,' shouted Scurry. 'He can't put himself together again. He's all mixed up in the water!'

'I did it all myself! I got rid of him!' sang Hurry. 'All by myself I did it.'

'You didn't. You couldn't have done it without me!' said Scurry. 'If I hadn't been a bucket you couldn't have put him into me when you made him change into water. You didn't do it all by yourself, so there!'

'Don't let's quarrel,' said Hurry. 'Oh, dear, Scurry, do you suppose it's all right to rinse my soapy clothes in the well water now that Crookity's all mixed up in it?'

'I don't know. We'll try,' said Scurry, and they raced home to get a bucket. They went to the well, filled it with water and carried it home between them.

And will you believe it, whenever the well water is used by anyone for washing, or whenever it is boiled in a kettle, it gurgles and sings in a curious watery voice that says, 'Crookity, crookity, crook, crookity, crookity, crook,' all the time.

I'd like to hear it – but I don't think I'd much like to use it. I wouldn't be surprised to find the water jumping out of the wash tub or the kettle and changing back into the goblin again!

It Grew and It Grew

It Grew and It Grew

ONCE LITTLE Fibs the pixie told his mother a story. He often didn't tell the truth and it made her sad.

Fibs had been playing with his ball in the garden and it had landed on the rose bed. He had gone to get it and had trodden all over the bed and broken some roses off.

'Oh, Fibs – did you do that?' cried his mother.

'No. It was Frisky the dog,' said Fibs.

'Then he's very naughty,' said his mother. 'Go and find him and tie him up.'

Fibs didn't want to do that. He liked Frisky. But he ran out and pretended to look for him. 'Mother, he's frightened and he's gone into the next-door garden,' he said when he came back. That was another fib, of course. That first fib was certainly growing!

'Oh, dear!' said his mother in dismay. 'Dame Pitpat has hens, and if Frisky chases them she will be so cross. Go and ask her if she will let you go into her garden and catch him.'

Fibs ran off. He went next door and pretended to ring the bell. Nobody came, of course, because he hadn't rung the bell. He ran back to his mother.

'Dame Pitpat is out,' he said. 'I rang and I rang and nobody came. But never mind – Frisky ran out of her garden and he's gone down the road.'

'Well, that's good,' said his mother. 'But I shall certainly tie him up when he comes in.'

She went into the garden to hang up some clothes. Fibs heaved a sigh of relief. Perhaps now he needn't tell another fib.

Soon his mother came hurrying in. 'Fibs, Fibs, where are you? There's a burglar in Dame Pitpat's house. There must be, because you said she was out. I distinctly saw someone at the upstairs window. You go and ask old Rappy to come along and find out!'

Fibs sighed. Oh, dear, oh, dear! It was all beginning again! He ran out to Mr Rappy's house, but he didn't knock at the door. He just stood there – then he went back again to his mother.

'Mr Rappy says he's got a very bad leg and he can't come. He says you must have been mistaken. There can't be a burglar in Dame Pitpat's house.'

'How does *he* know?' cried his mother. 'Well then, I shall send you to Mr Plod the policeman. *Somebody* must come and get the burglar next door! Run, Fibs, run and get Mr Plod at once.'

Fibs couldn't think what to do! He was standing there, wondering what to say, when his mother gave a loud cry. 'Oh! There is Mr Plod! Look, by the front gate. Go and get him at once!'

Fibs went out slowly, hoping that Mr Plod would have gone by the time he reached the gate. His mother ran out crossly. 'Why don't you hurry, Fibs? Mr Plod, Mr Plod! There's a robber in Dame Pitpat's house!'

Mr Plod turned in surprise. 'Is there really, ma'am? Then I'll climb in at a window and catch him right away!'

And in no time at all there was Mr Plod climbing in at a window of Dame Pitpat's house! There was nobody downstairs so he went upstairs very quietly and walked into the bedroom.

Somebody screamed and sat up in bed! It was Dame Pitpat herself, having a little rest. 'Oh, what is it? Who is it? Why, it's Mr Plod! What do you want, Mr Plod?'

'Well, I was told there was a burglar in the house,' said Mr Plod. 'Little Fibs next door was sent to you with a message and he came back and said you were out, and then his mother saw somebody moving in the upstairs room and ...'

'Bless us all! I wasn't out!' said Dame Pitpat. 'He couldn't have rung the bell or I'd have heard it.

It was me that Fibs's mother saw upstairs. Please go away, Mr Plod, and leave me in peace.'

Mr Plod went down and told Fibs's mother and she was really very puzzled. She was even more puzzled when she saw Mr Rappy coming out of his house with his stick under his arm, walking quickly to catch the bus.

'Why, Mr Rappy! When Fibs asked you for help just now, you told him you couldn't come because you had a very bad leg!' cried Fibs's mother, looking most amazed.

'Nonsense!' said Mr Rappy. 'He never came to ask me anything at all. Just one of his tales!'

'Fibs! You didn't go to Mr Rappy – and I don't believe you went to Dame Pitpat's either!' said his mother, shocked. 'And I don't suppose Frisky was in her garden. Where *is* he then? Frisky, Frisky!'

A loud barking came from upstairs. Fibs's mother ran up and opened a door. Inside the room was Frisky, wagging his tail.

'Why, he's been here all the time,' said Fibs's mother. 'He's been asleep on his rug. He *couldn't* have run over the rose bed and broken the roses. Then who did, Fibs? Answer me that!'

She went out to the rose bed – and there she saw the footprints quite clearly. They were Fibs's, of course.

'You horrid, mean little pixie!' she cried. 'Blaming poor Frisky – telling me he had run away next door – and saying that Dame Pitpat was out and Mr Rappy had a bad leg. Don't you know that one fib leads to another and always brings trouble in the end? Well, trouble is coming to you, Fibs!'

Poor Fibs! His mother told the truth – it was ages before he was allowed out to play again. It's strange how one fib leads to another, isn't it? Fibs knows that now and he'll never forget it!

Acknowledgements

All efforts have been made to seek necessary permissions.

The stories in this publication first appeared in the following publications:

'Binkle Has the Doctor' first appeared in *The Enid Blyton Book of Bunnies (Binkle & Flip)*, published by George Newnes in 1925.

'The Three Naughty Children' first appeared in *Enid Blyton's Sunny Stories for Little Folks*, No. 192, 1934.

'Mr Meddle Goes Out Shopping' first appeared as 'Mister Meddle Goes Out Shopping' in *Enid Blyton's Sunny Stories*, No. 160, 1940.

'The Squirrels and the Nuts' first appeared in *The Teachers World*, No. 1707, 1936.

'Peeko's Prank' first appeared in *The Teachers World*, No. 1175, 1926.

'The Story that Came True' first appeared in *Enid Blyton's Sunny Stories*, No. 452, 1949.

'The Bad Cockyolly Bird' first appeared in *Enid Blyton's Sunny Stories*, No. 32, 1937.

'Mother Minky's Trick' first appeared in *Enid Blyton's Sunny Stories*, No. 159, 1940.

'The Very Naughty Dog' first appeared in *The Teachers World*, No. 1399, 1930.

'Tiddley-Pom the Tailor' first appeared as 'Tiddley-Pom, the Tailor' in *Sunny Stories for Little Folks*, No. 55, 1928.

'The Little Girl Who Told Stories' first appeared in *Sunny Stories for Little Folks*, No. 76, 1929.

'He Bought a Secret' first appeared in *Enid Blyton's Sunny Stories*, No. 486, 1950.

'Thirty-Three Candles' first appeared as 'Thirty-three Candles' in *Enid Blyton's Sunny Stories*, No. 534, 1952.

'The Greedy Little Sparrow' first appeared in *Enid Blyton's Sunny Stories*, No. 74, 1938.

'The Magic Clock' first appeared in *Enid Blyton's Sunny Stories*, No. 169, 1940.

'The Little Tease' first appeared in *Enid Blyton's Magazine*, No. 20, Vol. 2, 1954.

'It Was the Wind!' first appeared in *Enid Blyton's Sunny Stories*, No. 443, 1948.

'Amelia Jane and the Soap' first appeared in *Enid Blyton's Sunny Stories*, No. 100, 1938.

'Here Comes the Wizard!' first appeared in *Enid Blyton's Sunny Stories*, No. 466, 1949.

'Mr Grumble-Grumps' first appeared as 'Mister Grumble-Grumps' in *Enid Blyton's Sunny Stories*, No. 59, 1938.

'The Sticky Gnome's Prank' first appeared in *Sunny Stories for Little Folk*, No. 195, 1934.

'Hallo! How Are You?' first appeared in *Enid Blyton's Magazine*, No. 19, Vol. 3, 1955.

'The Disappearing Hats' first appeared in *Enid Blyton's Sunny Stories*, No. 14, 1937.

'The Wizard's Watering Can' first appeared as 'The Wizard's Watering-Can' in *Sunny Stories for Little Folk*s, No. 178, 1933.

'Nobbly-One the Gnome' first appeared in *Sunny Stories for Little Folks*, No. 182, 1934.

'The Walking Bone' first appeared in *Sunny Stories for Little Folks*, No. 185, 1934.

'Goblin Magic' first appeared in *Enid Blyton's Sunny Stories*, No. 512, 1951.

'It Grew and It Grew' first appeared in *Enid Blyton's Sunny Stories*, No. 519, 1951.

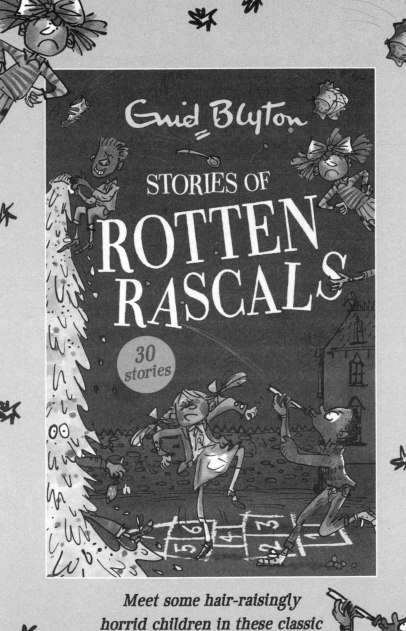

Enid Blyton

STORIES OF

ROTTEN
RASCALS

30
stories

Meet some hair-raisingly
horrid children in these classic
stories from the world's
best-loved storyteller!

Enid Blyton

is one of the most popular children's authors of all time. Her books have sold over 500 million copies and have been translated into other languages more often than any other children's author.

Enid Blyton adored writing for children. She wrote over 700 books and about 2,000 short stories. *The Famous Five* books, now 80 years old, are her most popular. She is also the author of other favourites including *The Secret Seven*, *The Magic Faraway Tree* and *Malory Towers*.

Born in London in 1897, Enid lived much of her life in Buckinghamshire and loved dogs, gardening and the countryside. She was very knowledgeable about trees, flowers, birds and animals.

Dorset – where some of the Famous Five's adventures are set – was a favourite place of hers too.

Enid Blyton's stories are read and loved by millions of children (and grown-ups) all over the world. Visit enidblyton.co.uk to discover more.